After losing his partner Toby, Chase faces a long, painful road back to life and love.

At first, he doesn't see how he can go on, but then Chase and Toby's old friend Mike cajoles him into returning to Chicago for the annual International Mr. Leather Competition. There Chase revisits a world of hot, casual sex that he had forgotten existed, meets a friend who cares more for him than he ever realized, and discovers the possibility that he just might be able to move on without betraying the memory of his late partner.

Will Chase find his way back once more to life? To love? And will he find that place he's been missing? *Home.* You'll have to experience the heartrending journey firsthand to find out.

I0583555

# HOMECOMING

*Rick R. Reed*

A NineStar Press Publication

www.ninestarpress.com

# Homecoming

Printed in the USA

Print ISBN: 978-1-64890-109-6

NineStar Press Edition, October, 2020
Originally Published in March 2011

Also available in eBook, ISBN: 978-1-64890-108-9

WARNING:

This book contains sexually explicit content, which may only be suitable for mature readers, and the death of a prominent character.

# Prologue

## "Love and Sex: Oil and Water?"

*How do we make love stay? How do we make lust stay? Heady questions...and if you're looking for answers, you've come to the wrong place. I'm just as mystified as you are.*

\*

I read somewhere, probably in one of those gay self-help books, that there are lots of gay men who can't unite love and sex. The book reasoned that because many gay men are so promiscuous and indulge in so many anonymous sex acts that the idea of love and sex become mutually exclusive. It's as though we compartmentalize the two. After you've blown a hundred guys with whom you might not even be on a first name basis, it's difficult to merge love, commitment, and friendship with blowing someone. Or at least that's how the reasoning goes.

I've been thinking about this lately and wondering if there's any validity to it. I mean, there does seem to be a correlation between the length of a couple's time together and the frequency of the sex they have (at least with each other). I have known many gay male couples who have been together for a long period of time and their interest in each other sexually seems to wane after a while. Conversely, their affection for each other, their mutual respect, their closeness, may even grow as their desire wanes.

Why is this?

Why would some of us (many, from what I've seen and experienced) prefer to take our corporeal pleasures with someone we hardly know over someone with whom we've decided we want to spend our lives? Has Western civilization simply confused the whole concept of romantic love and sexuality? Could it be that maybe the two do not go hand in hand, as books, movies, and fairy tales tell us? Is there something wrong with a gay couple who rarely has sex? Because the passion's gone, should they be looking elsewhere for a new partner, one with whom they can ignite the cycle of passion, coupling with bunny-like frequency, and the withering of that same desire all over again?

Is there the perfect man out there for each of us, one with whom we can enjoy everyday life as well as nights of passionate abandon...forever? Is it just that men are following some primal biological imperative to spread their seed to as many potential mates as possible?

Do gay men have lots of promiscuous sex because, like a balls-licking dog, they can?

I don't know the answers to any of the above questions. I've read here and there that monogamy is a ridiculous concept, one that sets itself up for failure because human beings are not designed to be monogamous. Being a gay man, living in a world rife with sexual possibilities makes the monogamy concept even harder to accept as a viable lifestyle choice. But then, why do or why would many of us feel so betrayed and jealous if we discover a partner's indiscretion? Even if our rational mind tells us that indiscretion had nothing to do with our partner's love for us and that it threatens our relationship not a whit?

Is there anything wrong with having a committed relationship with someone based on mutual interests, respect, caring, and the desire to build a home and a life together, even if sex doesn't figure into the equation? Does it make more sense to live in a wildly unstable, unsuitable relationship where the sex is always passionate? Which would you choose?

Can we have both? Are we only setting ourselves up for disappointment to expect both?

I don't know. Do you?

*(From the Tales from the Sexual Underground blog by Bryce Weston)*

# Chapter One

Toby tried his best to stay awake.

He was on the Microsoft shuttle, traveling home from his job at Microsoft's Redmond campus, to his condo in Seattle's Capitol Hill neighborhood. It was a long commute, but he had his phone, his weariness (which meant he sometimes slept through the trip), and an overactive imagination for company and entertainment. The commute was made longer because he had to transfer to a bus once he got to downtown Seattle to get close enough to home. Home was a two-bedroom with amazing views of the Space Needle and Lake Union he shared with his soul mate, his beloved, his special *one*, Chase.

He was grateful every single day for the wonderful life he'd built for himself. He was one of those lucky folks who could hardly imagine how things could possibly be any better.

The familiar scenery passed as the bus drew closer to closer to downtown.

He wished he could banish this fatigue, but it had been a long day and a long week and there simply wasn't much fuel left in his tank.

But it was his birthday, for god's sakes ! He wanted to celebrate—so much. It was a milestone, after all. One doesn't turn forty every day.

If he came home exhausted and ready for bed—and sleep—at nine o'clock, it would only validate the sinking feeling Toby had that forty was the beginning of the long path down that particular piece of geography known as "over the hill."

He hoped seeing Chase at the door to their shared home would revive him enough to at least maybe order a Pagliacci pizza for delivery and to stream a couple of episodes of *Unforgiven* on Britbox.

Now, that sounded like a perfect evening and a birthday celebration ideally suited to his introvert leanings. He was grateful once again he and Chase hadn't made big plans for the 4-0. They could have a nice dinner over the weekend, perhaps, at his favorite Korean street-food eatery, Revel, over in the Fremont neighborhood. Or maybe they'd splurge, as they had last year, and try to get a table at Canlis.

To keep himself awake, he brought his phone out of the pocket of his jeans and, like everyone else on the bus, stared down at the illuminated screen.

He checked Facebook and found it flooded with birthday wishes, so many he got lost in the long thread of well wishes, emojis, and memes exhorting him to have an amazing celebration. Twitter was a little less celebratory, but he still felt like a rock star when he scrolled through all the birthday tweets directed toward him.

Last, he brought up one of his favorite blogs, *Tales from the Sexual Underground*, written by an old friend of his from Chicago, Danny Britton, who went by the more youthful-sounding pen name of Bryce Weston, because Danny didn't know how seriously he'd be taken as a middle-aged dude from Highland Park writing about fringe sexual practices and personages. No one would guess most of his tales were made-up (except for the interviews with sex workers and porn stars) and that the man behind the blog was actually pushing fifty and was happily settled with a doctor husband and two very demanding Pomeranians. The wildest Danny got was a season ticket to Ravinia music park every summer.

Danny posted a new column twice a week and devoted the other days to curated roundups of news about sex workers, the porn industry, and the rights and freedoms of those wanting to pursue kinks without government interference. His blog had grown so popular that, last Toby heard, he was making a good chunk of change from advertising. The Twitter followers for his blog numbered in the tens of thousands.

He had a way of writing that made Toby feel he was speaking directly to him, even though he and Chase were pretty much mere acquaintances when they all lived back in the Windy City area.

This week's latest blog post, for example, spoke to him and where he found himself in life at age forty perfectly. He'd read it earlier on his lunch break, but found himself wanting to savor its short, sweet, sexy words one more time. It was all about how love wins out over sex every time, although the two together could actually induce heaven on earth, provided everything was in place.

It was amazing how Danny could put himself in the shoes of a *single* gay man so convincingly. He'd been with his physician partner, Jake Wells, for more than two decades.

Back when he and Chase lived in Chicago, he'd tease Danny about the blog when they'd run into him at Wrigley Field or strolling around Millennium Park or at the gay beach at Ardmore and Hollywood. Toby would wonder aloud if Danny had been reincarnated from the soul of a wanton slut of a gay man, or if he was perhaps a horndog trapped in a gay milquetoast's body.

Perhaps inspired by the teasing, Danny had even written a blog about *that*. It was hilarious. You never knew what would inspire Danny, or Bryce, as he was known to the masses.

Anyway, this particular post, though, made him so grateful and happy he'd found his one and only, Chase. He was grateful there was no longer any need to play the field. Someone, a happily married gay friend of his at Microsoft, had once quipped that there was no reason to go out for hamburger when he had filet mignon at home.

Toby couldn't agree more. He began reading.

## "Going for Quality, Not Quantity"

Why, I can remember a time when sex parties and the filthy backrooms of leather bars were the height of sexual euphoria. Coupling with strangers en masse set my heart to racing, the blood to pumping, and the brain to disengaging. Caution and even reason were thrown to the wind. Out the window too—unwisely, yes—went fears of AIDS, STIs, and even the limitations of the human lumbar system as I swam through the darkness like a hungry fish, searching with eyes glazed for the next cock, mouth, or ass.

But all of that stuff seems to have lost its charm, to be replaced by "gasp!" if not romance, then at least human connection.

Am I getting old? Maybe not. Maybe I've just grown jaded. And, wonder of wonders, perhaps I've grown wiser.

But these days, sex seems hotter when it's one-on-one, with someone I actually know more about than the fact that he's able to swing that baseball cap around effortlessly, inhale a bottle of poppers, and blow me all at the same time. I get more aroused in my own bed, waiting for someone whose name, occupation, and likes and dislikes I at least have a rudimentary knowledge of than I used to lining up for a crack at the crack in the sling.

A couple cases in point. Old habits die hard, which is why I readily accepted an invitation to a party held during International Mr. Leather (IML) weekend in one of the rooms of the host hotel, the Hyatt. There were to be about fifteen guys gathered. There would be no chips and salsa, witty repartee, or flirtatious glances across the room. No, we all knew what we were there for. The only party favors supplied were bottles of various lube (even that new sensation J Lube, which bears no relation to J Lo, except that both might or might not have something to do with big asses, but I digress), poppers, a sling set up in one corner of the room, and a portable enema hose in the bathroom's shower. There was no music. No conversation. Just naked men (and some pretty hot ones), grunts, groans, and the odd operatic aria ("Sweet mystery of life, I adore you").

After about an hour or so, and making the corporeal acquaintance of at least five other men, the whole thing seemed rather amusing and well, if I'm honest, a little boring. Gatherings like these were often so much better in the imagination than they were in real life.

So I left, even though the partiers had hours to go before they slept. Trying to get my clothes back on amidst a tableau out of something Fellini might have dreamed up was no easy task. Picking my way to the door through the sweaty bodies almost made me giggle...it was like playing a very grown up game of Twister.

Contrast that with Sunday...and a very nice day at the beach with someone whom I'm getting to know on many levels. Contrast the sex party with just the two of us, in my sun-drenched bedroom, pretty much doing what the guys at the sex party were doing, but instead of looking for who we should fuck next, we stared into each other's eyes, charting the course of each other's pleasure.

What's happened to me? Does this mean I've finally grown up? Or am I just getting boring?

Yeah, Toby thought, I get it. He and Chase had been together now for years, and the thought of wanting a little variety or a little on the side had no appeal at all for Toby. He'd won the prize—a hot man who still inspired his passion, but also one who inspired a sense of contentment, a sense of home, and best of all, an assured future together.

They were almost at his stop and, yes, Toby, anticipating kissing Chase in the next few minutes gave him with a boost of energy. He wouldn't need anyone else to make his fortieth birthday one for the books.

# Chapter Two

Everything was ready for the surprise party.

Chase had decorated their Seattle condo with gold, purple, and white streamers and matching balloons, giving the place a Mardi Gras feel. A specially made banner hung above the old oak pedestal dining room table with Toby's high school graduation photo and the words, "Over the Hill? Hardly! Happy 40th, Toby!" emblazoned across its slick white surface. The hutch near the table, a distressed piece rescued from someone's garbage and lovingly painted chromium yellow by Toby, was piled high with wrapped presents. Chase had gone a little overboard, but Toby was worth it.

He always would be. He was Chase's heart and one couldn't live without that particular organ.

Their condo, in Seattle's Capitol Hill neighborhood, was alive with the electricity of anticipation. Even what lay outside the windows—overlooking the Space Needle and downtown Seattle—appeared to be lit up for a party this early spring evening. Late afternoon sunlight sparkled on Lake Union's blue/green waters as a seaplane landed on its surface.

Chase had curated a special birthday party playlist that included songs from across the board. There was everything from Lesley Gore's "It's My Party" to Katy Perry's "Birthday" to Conway Twitty's "Happy Birthday, Darlin'." The list was rounded out with a whole bunch of dance, trance, and disco, all pulled from Toby's club-haunting days, back when they'd lived in Chicago and busted moves on the dance floor at Roscoe's.

Chase had gathered almost all of Toby's friends for the bash, swearing them to secrecy and getting them in on the weeks-long planning for his partner's milestone birthday.

Now, they were spread out throughout the kitchen, dining, and living areas, clutching cocktails in their hands, chattering about Toby and how he looked too young to actually be forty, and how surprised he would be when he walked in the door. It was a broad cross-section of people from Toby's work, his volunteer gig at Lifelong AIDS Alliance, where he worked in the kitchen on Wednesdays, to members of his gay men's book club, The Violet Quill. Toby knew a lot of people and it was a testimony to his kindness and charisma that so many had shown up for the bash. The excitement in the little two-bedroom was electric, almost palpable.

Chase himself relished the idea of Toby's handsome face wide-eyed in surprise and delight. He knew Toby wasn't big on parties, but Chase couldn't let Toby's milestone birthday slip by without pulling out all the stops. He'd want Toby to do the same for him when he passed over the threshold into his forties, which was still a couple of years away.

Chase bustled around the condo, making sure the hors d'oeuvres were in place. The dining room table was laden with bowls of Pad Thai and Panang Curry, Jasmine rice, pot stickers, chicken satay with peanut sauce, and prawns enveloped in wonton wrappers, all bought from their favorite Thai place on Broadway. Chase had dusted the tablecloth with purple glitter. He could just picture

Toby's face—the short blond hair, the wide-set blue eyes, the finely chiseled features—alive with total shock and pleasure at everything Chase had assembled to celebrate his special day.

The food and the local friends weren't the only things Chase couldn't wait for Toby to see.

Diagonal to the dining room table, Chase had a bar set up, sparing no expense to have it stocked with top-shelf liquor, wine, beer, and mixers. And the bartender was yet another in a long line of surprises Chase had arranged. The guy was pure eye candy—Latino with olive skin, buzzed black hair, the darkest eyes Chase had ever seen, and ripped and bulging muscles that should have put him on the cover of a fitness magazine rather than behind a bar. These were visible because his outfit consisted only of tight black pants and red suspenders. Best part was that the guy seemed truly affable and friendly. His excitement at Toby's arrival did not seem in the least faked.

And the biggest and best surprise of all stood in the corner by the windows with the view they had bought the place for. Mike. Chase had been thrilled when Toby's old best friend from Chicago had agreed to fly out for the party. Mike and Toby went back years, to their college days at Miami University in Oxford, Ohio. When Chase and Toby lived in the Windy City, he had to admit to himself that he would be lying if he said he wasn't jealous of the two men's closeness, but Mike had always seemed genuinely happy that Toby had found Chase, after years of searching for *the one* in and out of leather bars all over Chicago's north side. Mike was simply a good guy, handsome but unaware of his appeal, with an easy laugh, and always willing to help out in any situation. The fact that he remained single was a mystery to Chase, but Toby would always explain his status away with a wave of his hand. "He's a sweetheart, but a bit of a man-whore. Too many fish in the sea to sample. I don't know if he'd be constitutionally able to settle down with just one guy." And Chase would never fail to ask, even though he already knew the answer, "But you're not like that, right? You're happy you settled down with just one?"

And Toby always responded with a smile and a nudge. "Well, you never know. You'll do, though, until the right one comes along." And then he would make a lie of his words by soulfully kissing Chase and erasing any and all doubt Toby might have about his status as *the one* in Toby's life.

Although Toby had left the leather scene behind—and sold off his chaps, harness, and bar vest on Craigslist—Mike had never gotten away from it, which was evident even now. Mike was tall, verging on six five, with buzzed salt-and-pepper hair, a matching beard, pale-gray eyes, and a deep tan. In another life, Chase would have gone weak in the knees at the sight of this hunk. Now, he seemed more like a loving brother-in-law. But once he had arrived at their condo from Sea-Tac Airport earlier that day, in jeans and a Bears T-shirt, he had changed into full leather regalia for the party—tight black leather jeans, a clinging T-shirt that showed off his ripples and bulges to good advantage, leather vest, and combat boots. He looked like some sort of Tom of Finland fantasy. Chase had wanted to close the mouths of the other gay male guests as Mike walked by. One of the things that made Mike so damn cute was the fact that he always seemed blissfully unaware of his allure, which just upped the ante of his attractiveness.

Right now, it appeared Chase was just one of a growing legion of fans for Mike. The leather man had a full entourage of new friends gathered around him, all Seattle men, dressed in their usual garb of sweat shirts, fleece, jeans, and, even in March, sandals (some with socks, but that was Seattle for you). It seemed like a game—almost all of them vying to catch Mike's dizzying pale-eyed stare or a chance to chat with him.

Chase hurried over to Mike and managed to pull him away from the crowd of fawning admirers that had gathered around him. The two men stood near the front door. Chase eyed Mike. "So are you excited?"

"Oh God, yes. It's been how long since we've all gotten together?" Mike asked. "Seems like forever." His voice was gravelly, deep, a bit of Barry White. It alone could send an electric pulse right to just about gay man's (or straight woman's) nether regions.

Chase thought about their last time together—he and Toby had been back to Chicago about four years ago, when they returned to the city in August, in miserable heat, to visit Mike and go to the Halsted Market Days street festival. They'd rented the top of a two-flat in the city's Andersonville neighborhood, to be close both to the bars on Clark and the gay beach to the east. The street fair had been crowded with sweaty bodies pressing against each other, rainbow flags, leather and twinks, vendor booths, bar booths, and a crush of people of all different sizes, shapes, colors, and orientations. It had been a fun time, but both Toby and Chase were ready to return to Seattle's cool temps and summer sunshine by the end of that week, a sure sign that Seattle had usurped Chicago as "home."

This trip was Mike's first to Seattle. He planned on staying a week and came prepared with a whole lineup of things to do and see—the Space Needle, of course, Pike Place Market, yes, but also bars like the Cuff and day trips to hike in the pristine Cascade Mountains. He'd come with a full list of restaurants to check out, planning on taking full advantage of the city's reputation as a culinary capital, especially when it came to things like Asian cuisine and seafood.

Chase brought himself back to the present and answered Mike, "It's simply been too damn long, Mike. A good four years! We miss you all the time. It seems like not a day goes by that Toby doesn't wish we lived closer. I mean, we adore Seattle, but Chicago—and you—always have a huge place in both of our hearts."

Mike shook his head, smiling. "That long, huh? We should never let that happen again. No excuse for it." He pulled Chase close in a bear hug. "You guys mean too much to me to see you so infrequently."

Chase pulled away, a little breathless. He grunted, "Promise. We'll both make a better effort. Toby and I were even thinking of a trip out to Chi-town in the fall." The guy didn't know his own strength; he'd almost squeezed Chase to death. Not that Chase minded—in fact, the truth was he was a little turned on by Mike's closeness and brute force—but here he was, waiting for his lover to come home to the surprise party he had spent the last several weeks of his life planning. He looked over the room, which had gone hushed, with several people moving to the windows to peer outside.

He turned back to Mike, glancing down at his watch. It was a quarter to seven. "Of course, it's just my luck that Toby's late for his own party! I don't know where that man is; he's usually home by six fifteen at the latest." Chase rolled his eyes. "Work!"

"He'll be here," Mike said, grinning. "Probably just got tied up." His eyes went faraway. "I can just picture it."

Chase punched his shoulder. "Cut it out! I know what you're picturing." Just then, he felt the vibration and then heard the ring tone he had set up just for Toby on his cell phone. He pulled the device out of his pocket and glanced at Mike. "Speak of the devil."

He pressed Accept. "Hey honey. Get held up at the office?" Toby worked at Microsoft as a technical writer and the days could often get really long, especially when one figured in the commute from the campus in suburban Redmond, along with the usual—and horrendous—Seattle traffic.

"Yeah. I won't bore you with the details. Sorry I didn't call you sooner. I just wanted to get out of there, and then I fell asleep on the bus. I guess I really am forty! No energy!"

"Well, we'll fix that when you get home."

"What's for dinner?"

"Leftovers. We still had chili left from Wednesday night."

"Sounds good. And Chase?"

"Yeah?"

"I'm glad you're respecting my wishes to not do anything special for my birthday. I really do just want a quiet evening at home with the man I love. That to me is heaven. The perfect way to welcome in my forties."

Chase thought he'd get that quiet later, when they were asleep and everyone had gone home. But for now, as he looked around at the festive apartment and the anticipating guests, he didn't question going against Toby's wishes. He looked around at the throng, grateful they had all gone quiet when his cell phone rang. Someone had even been thoughtful enough to pause the playlist of party music going. He felt the tiniest twinge of doubt, though, hoping Toby would truly be thrilled—and not disappointed or angry with him—for planning this shindig.

After all, how many times does a guy turn forty?

"You know I love you, honey." Chase looked at Mike, who had an expectant expression on his face. "So where are you? Close?"

"Better. I'm just stepping off the bus." Chase heard the punctuation of the hiss of the pneumatic doors closing and the bass of the bus's engine as it roared off. The drop-off was just at the corner.

Surprise party time was almost here!

Toby said, "I can stop and pick up some cornbread from that bakery on Olive if you want, it would go great with—"

Chase's blood went cold at the sudden ceasing of Toby's words. It wasn't just silence he heard, but a sharp intake of breath, screeching brakes, a blaring horn, a bit of static and then...

Nothing.

Chase felt as though his heart had stopped. What had just happened? Surely, Toby had simply dropped his phone or something. His cell would ring again in a minute, and Toby would pick up where he'd left off. He'd laugh about his tendency to be a klutz. And then bemoan that they'd have to go to the Apple store out at University Village to replace the screen he'd surely cracked—again.

But the cell phone didn't ring. And with a feeling like he was moving in slow motion, Chase began to move toward the window that overlooked their street. He had heard the screeching brakes and horn more than just through the phone, he thought with a nauseating sense of dread. Bile splashed the back of his throat. His breath quickened.

He barely heard Mike calling after him, "Chase? What's the matter? You just went white as a ghost."

Outside, there were sirens in the distance. Outside, the traffic stopped in the street below them. Outside, a crumpled figure lay in the middle of the road, still. A woman stood nearby, her SUV door open, weeping.

That figure—the one lying twisted on the pavement—that wasn't Toby, was it?

It couldn't be. Chase peered through the darkness and knew that it was, but something inside him refused to believe it. *No, that's not my Toby. It couldn't be. I've told him a dozen times, at least, to pay attention and look where he's going when he's outside on his cell.*

Chase sat down suddenly, and hard, on the floor, staring numbly at the concerned faces of his friends as the sirens outside grew deafening.

For a moment, his mind, all on its own, went elsewhere. He was living in a dream, one where Toby was whole and in front of him. Forget a dream—it was a memory. One of their first dates and Toby, shy, had him over to his apartment in the Edgewater neighborhood of Chicago.

*He'd been so nervous about cooking for Chase. It was so sweet how he fussed over the dinner he'd made for them. Chase could see him wondering if the food and atmosphere would be good enough to impress him.*

*There were taper candles on Toby's little round oak pedestal table. A vase filled with irises and white lilies. And the dinner had been one of the best Chase had ever had—halibut poached in butter, dusted with flat-leaf parsley, orzo in a little garlic, olive oil, and lemon zest. Hot rolls. A salad of arugula and grapefruit sections. A crisp white—Chenin blanc?*

*They'd eyed each other across the table, Toby barely eating, testing Chase's reaction to the food.*

*At one point, Toby raised a glass. "We forgot to toast. So here's this—to many more dinners together."*

*They clinked glasses and Chase said, stupidly, "I'll drink to that. You keep cooking the same and you won't be able to get rid of me."*

*"Never," Toby had whispered. Fearing he'd said too much, he looked down, gulping his wine.*

And then reality stepped back in.

Horror.

Loss.

This couldn't be happening.

# Chapter Three

Toby burst through the front door, a little breathless. Jokingly, he cried, "Honey, I'm home!" He often yelled this out when he came home from work. Although the line was as corny as could be, it never failed to crack Toby up. Chase always rolled his eyes, but couldn't help but laugh too as he got caught up in Toby's delight with his own wit.

This time, though, Toby didn't snicker because delighted shock cut off his laughter at the knees. His jaw dropped.

"Surprise!" The assembled party guests cried out as one. There was laughing, cheering, and applause.

Toby took a stunned step back toward the still-open front door. At last, he let loose a short bark of surprised laughter. And then, Chase noticed, tears filled his eyes.

"Oh you guys! No." He shook his head, eyeing all the decorations, the friendly faces, the stack of presents, the hot bartender...and Mike, all the way from Chicago. "You shouldn't have. Really, it's too much." He seemed awestruck, confused, and delighted all at once.

He retreated farther back until he was outside the door, stooped over, and sobbing.

"Aw, babe, it's all for you..." Chase stood at the ready to lead Toby back into the condo and his birthday party.

It took several minutes for Chase to return to reality. He did so grudgingly, his breath heaving, and his eyes clouded by tears.

He looked up, dazed, at his and Toby's friends gathered around, all doing things like biting their lips, wringing their hands, turning to one another, thinking probably the person standing nearby had a better idea of what to say or do. No one could think of anything more intelligent to say than "Oh my God!" and "This is horrible!"

But what *does* one say under such circumstances?

Those who weren't staring at Chase, jockeyed for position at the street-facing window. Chase shuddered at their frantic whispers. He got up slowly from the floor, hoping against hope he'd made a mistake. His eyes, of course, had played a cruel trick on him. "Is it him? Is it Toby? Is he okay?"

Dully, Chase turned, staring at the different faces all craning toward the window, trying to see. He shook his head, as though to free it from mental cobwebs. For a moment, he wasn't sure where he was, even though his surroundings couldn't have been more familiar.

*Is this what shock feels like?* He couldn't remember the preceding few minutes of his life.

*What just happened?*

It was weird. There were moments he could remember, everyone talking at once, and for some reason all Chase could hear was white noise. Their mouths moved, but Chase couldn't hear any individual words, just a deafening static.

And why was everyone gawking at him now, as though they had never seen him before, like he was some sort of animal who had gotten inside the condo and they were wondering how to handle it? Some looked sad. Some looked alarmed. Others looked as though they were wondering when he would do something or say something to make everything make sense.

He lowered himself down to the floor once more, not sure his knees could support him. He'd never experienced faintness like this before; he'd never really known what it meant when folks said they'd gone *weak in the knees*—until now.

Mike squatted beside him, holding a glass of water in one hand, his other hand perched on Chase's shoulder. His gray eyes were alive with concern, his gaze twitching from the window above them, back to Chase. "Chase, bud, are you okay?" He held the glass out to him, but Chase waved it away. "You want something stronger?" He got up and moved to the bar. In seconds, he was back with what looked like another glass of water. "It's vodka. Drink it."

Chase did. The alcohol's burn was scant comfort. *There's no comfort in the world now...*

It all began to rush back in, the memory of the last few moments, starting with the phone call, when the buzzer from downstairs sounded. It made Chase jump and emit a little cry, the metallic bark was so sudden and loud. He tried to scramble to his feet to respond to its call. Mike pushed him back down to the floor. "Just stay put, buddy. Let someone else get it."

Chase slumped back, not thinking, not *wanting* to think, as Mike stood, pressing his face and one hand against the window's glass. Somebody, the redhead from Toby's fencing club, Chase thought, moved to the intercom on the wall. *What's his name? Brian? Ryan? Walter?* Chase didn't want to understand the import of the short conversation that took place.

"Yes?"

The voice coming through was deep, metallic, the voice of a robot. Sure, it was a robot. "Seattle Police Department. Can I come up, sir?"

"Gimme a second." The redhead pressed the button that would admit the cop to their building.

The whole condo went silent.

All of them were listening, Chase supposed, for the officer's footfalls on the staircase, for the hollow knock moments away. Chase felt bile splash at the back of his throat and tried once more to get up.

*This is not happening.*

Once again, Mike tried to get him to sit back down, this time on the couch, but Chase could allow no one else to answer the door. *This is my job. It's my job to hear the news, to take it, to understand it. Oh God, please no!*

When the knock sounded, Chase screamed. He leapt to his feet, rushing toward the door, a sick sense of inevitability swirling in his gut like a whirlpool.

Something caused him to pause in his tracks. He returned to the window, staring down at the street. The crowd had begun to disperse. The figure on the ground was gone and an EMT was just slamming the door to the back of the ambulance.

Chase's heart stopped for a minute as the lights atop the ambulance went on, swirling blue and red. He watched and cringed when a second knock came. The ambulance sped away.

Its siren did not wail.

Stiffly, Chase moved closer to the door to answer the knock, which now came a third time. The crowd in the apartment, who just such a short time ago were laughing and chattering to one another, excited, had grown somber and still. No one said a word. They parted, making room for Chase as he headed toward the door.

Chase reminded himself to unbolt the deadlock, to place his hand on the doorknob and turn it. He looked at the Seattle police officer standing outside. He was so young! He couldn't possibly be old enough to be on the force—rosy cheeks, baby smooth skin, a blond buzz cut. Dark blue eyes, almost the same shade of cobalt as his uniform. He looked like he belonged in high school, on the tennis team or something. And he appeared scared out of his mind.

For a moment, Chase felt sorry for him.

And then, Chase had a sudden urge to laugh at the sober expression that pulled the Cupid's bow of the officer's lips down. This boy/man trying to look serious was simply absurd. Baby Huey in law enforcement.

Chase blurted, "What do you want?"

"Sir, is this the home of Toby Grant?"

"Who wants to know?" Chase asked and he did begin to chuckle, just a little.

"Sir, this is the address we have for Toby Grant."

"Yes, this is his home. What of it, copper?" Chase snapped, not sure why he was acting this way. "Or do you prefer flatfoot? 5-0?" A giggle escaped his lips like a hiccup.

"What's your relationship to Mr. Grant, sir?"

"What's it to you?" Chase spat. And then his mind flickered to the *Mary Tyler Moore Show* and its Mr. Grant. He covered his mouth to stifle the laughter. "We're *lovers*, big homosexual lovers. It's the latest thing!"

Mike moved up beside him. He placed a hand on his shoulder and squeezed gently. "Officer, this is Chase Fullerton; he's Mr. Grant's partner. They both live here."

The officer nodded and exchanged a look with Chase. He cocked his head.

Chase could see the discomfort on the officer's face. The officer spoke quickly, almost as if he were reading from a prepared statement. *His delivery could use some work.*

"Sir, I'm sorry to have to inform you that Toby Grant was hit by a car outside." The officer looked down at the floor for a long moment; then his blue eyes met Chase's. "He did not survive the pedestrian vehicle collision."

"What?" Chase felt Mike's hand on his shoulder again and shrugged it away. "What are you trying to tell me? I don't understand."

"Mr. Grant expired on the scene, sir."

Chase laughed then, loud, hard, laughed until his sides ached, until he gripped the doorframe for support. "Expired? Like a library book? Or a carton of milk? Or maybe a coupon for Fred Meyer? Expired?" Chase laughed again, hard. "Yeah, that's a good one!"

He turned back to Mike, whose eyes were filling with tears. "Did you hear that, Mike? Officer Baby Huey here says that Toby 'expired' on the scene." Chase laughed some more, high-pitched, almost a titter. "That's a good one." He turned back to the officer. "A real knee-slapper. Tell me another."

The officer gave him a lost look, shrugged, and turned to go down the stairs. "I'm sorry for your loss," he said over his shoulder.

Toby's mouth was open, poised to make another quip, but Mike gripped him, turning him back toward the apartment. He called his thanks out to the descending officer's back and closed the door.

Chase couldn't stop laughing. "You know what's going on here, don't you?"

Mike led him to the couch and pressed him gently into its leather cushions. Chase continued, between bursts of breathless laughter. "Toby's just getting back at me. He knew I'd do something like this party, and this is all one big joke. He hates parties. I knew I shouldn't have thrown this one. Sure, he's getting his revenge." Chase collapsed into the couch, laughing until he could barely catch his breath, until tears poured down his cheeks. He screamed, "Nobody's expired! Nobody! People don't expire!"

Then he stopped and whispered, "They die." Chase bowed his head. His hands looked like someone else's. "Oh my God," he whispered.

He allowed himself a glance over at Mike, who had sat next to him, one arm protectively wrapped around him.

"My Toby's gone." The words came out as a strangled, hoarse cry.

Seemingly out of nowhere, the tears and the sobs came, choking, nearly suffocating. Mike wrapped his arms around Chase, holding him tight, one hand stroking his back. Chase gripped him, fingers digging into Mike's flesh so hard it had to hurt, but Mike didn't complain, and what else could Chase do? The pain was so deep, so real, visceral. He didn't know if a physical pain could be any worse. He buried his face in Mike's T shirt, trying to quell the hiccupping breath, the snot and the tears that all seemed ceaseless now that it had sunk in.

Toby was gone. Dead. *Not* expired.

How could this have happened? Chase wondered. He managed to pull away, eyes burning, sniffling. The condo was still set up for the party—all the balloons and streamers, the bar, the buffet. *How does a guy step off a bus, vibrant, happy, relatively young, and with his whole life ahead of him, suddenly, in a single moment just be...gone?*

A new round of sobs escaped as he watched their friends scurrying to grab coats from the pile on the bed and to depart, mumbling and whispering shocked words of condolence, some saying nothing. What was there to say, anyway? The bartender was shrugging into a shirt and gathering up his things to go as well.

In minutes the place was empty, and he was alone with Mike. He managed to stop sobbing after a while, and was even able to sit up, separate from Mike. There was a dull ache behind his eyes and the tears flowed now of their own accord. Chase barely noticed them.

"What do I do now? Do we need to go somewhere, identify the body? What do people do?"

Mike brushed a hand across his face, pressed his thumbs into the area below Chase's eyes to stem the flow of tears. "We do whatever we need to. I'll be here to help and support you every step of the way." Mike bit his lower lip; Chase could see he was trying not to cry.

"Wait!" Chase exclaimed. "Wait! You never got to see him. You came all this way and spent all that money." He sucked in a strangled breath. "And you never got to see your friend." It was tragic!

Mike drew him closer. "It's okay."

"No, it's not. It's so far from okay. I know how much Toby would have loved seeing you. It was my big surprise, Mike! He talked about you all the time. Now, he'll never have the chance to reconnect." Chase grabbed a throw pillow and hugged it to himself, rocking and regarding Mike out of the corner of his eye. "It isn't fair."

"I know."

The two men sat in silence for a long time. Water dripped from the faucet in the kitchen sink. The Friday night roar of traffic, mufflers, horns honking sounded outside. There was the thump of footsteps upstairs, a snatch of unintelligible conversation, laughter. Music started up. Lady Gaga?

How could the world just go on? Didn't they know? How could they pretend everything was normal?

After a while, Chase turned to Mike. "I have to see him. I have to see him. Do you get it?" He was nearly breathless.

"Of course, I do. We'll go down to the hospital; we'll take a look."

Chase stood suddenly. "I have to see him now. Right now." He began pacing. An idea had emerged from the fog in his brain. "Maybe they were wrong. Maybe he *isn't* dead. You know, they could have revived him in the ambulance or maybe in the ER? Maybe they used those paddle things on him and restarted his heart!"

"Chase..." Mike stood beside him.

"It all happened so fast, Mike. Maybe he even came to in the ambulance. Maybe he'd had one of those 'near death' experiences and they sent him back because it wasn't his time."

Chase gnawed on a hangnail, pondering. "It can't be over like that." He snapped his fingers to illustrate the point. Toby had lived too long. He was too important to Chase for him to simply die in the blink of an eye. A stupid accident, not watching where he was going as he crossed the street was too mundane a way to die. Ridiculous!

"Not just like that. Not so, so...fast." He wiped his nose with the back of his hand and summoned up a smile for Mike. "He's *not* dead. He can't be. There has to be more. A person doesn't simply step off a bus and..." Chase's words trailed off into silence.

Mike waited.

Finally, Chase said, "Let's go see him. I need to see him."

"I'll get our coats. Why don't you go splash some water on your face? Take a minute. I'll call and see where they've taken him."

Chase started toward the little powder room adjacent to the living area. He froze and turned back to Mike as something occurred to him. "What am I going to do with his gift? I spent two week's pay on a new watch for him. It was beautiful, a Movado with a diamond, the nicest thing I ever gave him." Chase looked at Mike, helpless.

Mike came to him, wrapped his arms around him once more and held him close, whispering, his lips inches away from Chase's ear. "We'll give it to him, sweetheart. He can still have it. Now go get yourself together."

"And let's go see Toby." Chase disappeared into the bathroom, and Mike went to gather up their coats.

# Chapter Four

Chase stood outside his condo's front door, too tired to open it. The day had been endless, exhausting, drawing on reserves Chase never knew he possessed. He touched the dark mahogany-stained door, tracing his fingers around the brass knocker that hung in the center.

*

*"You're gonna love this place," Ian Vincent, their realtor, had told them just before opening the door for the first time. It was their first day of house-hunting and only the second place they were seeing. The first had been a run-down disaster in the Eastwood neighborhood. "There's already interest, so if you like it, I'd suggest we put in an offer right away."*

*"We haven't even seen the place yet! Just open the door," Toby had snapped. Patience was never one of his virtues.*

*But when he opened the door and they looked straight ahead through the large windows, they were sold. Lake Union shimmered, the sunlight dancing on its waters like diamonds. A sea plane was just touching down on its surface. The Space Needle rose up before them, iconic.*

*"We'll take it," Chase had blurted before they'd even crossed the threshold.*

*"What he's doing, you know, is trying to put us in a good place for negotiations. By seeming less-than-interested, he's certain to drive down our initial offer." Toby was all sarcasm, but the delight on his face matched Chase's excitement.*

*It wasn't just the stunning views.*

*It was home. Chase knew it in his heart, and he was certain Toby did too.*

\*

Back in the present, Chase didn't know if he even had enough strength left to simply reach down and turn the knob. He let his head drop so it hit the door, *thunk*, seriously considering letting himself slide down to the floor, to curl up and spend the night there. He didn't know if he could bear going inside again.

What was inside, anyway? An empty condo, a shell where once there had been life, love, happiness, a future...a home. All of that was gone now. The furniture within, the electronics, the stainless steel appliances in the kitchen, even that coveted view of the Space Needle, were all now nothing more than things, relics of a bygone time. They might as well have been props on a stage set. What was a home anyway without the people you loved in it? Simply a dwelling.

He sighed, told himself he'd had enough of his own nonsense. *Stop feeling sorry for yourself!* He fished his ring of keys from his pocket, opened the door, and slipped inside.

He debated again—simple decisions had suddenly become so hard—this time whether he should turn on any lights. The darkness was a kind of comfort. With just the light from the street shining in the windows, he could almost believe he was getting home late and that Toby slumbered in the bedroom and would awake to give him a sleepy kiss as Chase undressed next to the bed. It was one of those mundane moments Chase had experienced so many times before, now it was precious, fragile, a relic.

Finally, he moved across the living room and turned on a small Mica-shaded desk lamp that stood atop an antique secretary desk. It gave the room a warm, amber glow, just enough light for Chase to see well enough to pour himself a tumbler of vodka. He rarely drank anything straight, but the burn of the alcohol and the way its warmth filled his gut seemed fitting after the day he'd had.

He sat on the leather couch, kicked off his dress shoes, and put his feet up on the glass and chrome coffee table, feeling, in addition to weary, utterly alone. The feeling extended much further than simply being here, in their home. All day, Chase felt as though he walked the streets of Seattle as a sort of ghost, isolated from everyone else, his grief an invisible barrier.

Mike had taken a late afternoon flight back to Chicago. He insisted on getting himself to the airport, even though Chase offered to give him a lift. "It's a long way out to Sea-Tac," he'd weakly protested, and Mike had countered with, "Honey, I'll just hop on the light rail. No worries about traffic and it's super cheap. I'm a big boy." He'd smiled and like an Italian nonna, had pinched Chase's cheek before kissing it goodbye.

Toby's parents and his sister, Elaine, had opted for a taxi to Sea-Tac. They weren't as experienced with traveling as Mike and the idea of grabbing a bus to the light rail and then the public train seemed daunting. Chase told them to stay cool in Phoenix and then, in

Toby's mom's arms, had wept once more, even though he felt his own grief well had run dry.

Chase's mom, Annette, had left earlier that day for her flight back to Pittsburgh. She had taken his face in her hands just before she left, her greenish-brown eyes searching his own, searching for his pain so she could put a Band-Aid on it. A mother's way. "You take care of yourself now. And remember, you can always come home if you need to. Your old room is always there and waiting for you." She'd sucked in a quivering breath. "I know you're a grown man, but I'd love the chance to take care of you again, if only for a little while. I can make you pastina with egg, cheese, and butter, just like I did when you were little. It's always your home, you know."

Chase had managed, somehow, to hold himself together at this farewell.

*Home.* That word again. Chase wondered if it would ever have the import it once did.

Everyone he loved was now far away...or dead. Chase dismissed a mental image that rose up, Toby on that steel table in the morgue, his skin drained white, bruised. He wished he had a way to excise that memory from his brain forever.

*It isn't him. It's a husk, a suit of clothes my Toby wore.*

*Don't, just don't. You don't need to get even more morose now. You've had enough feeling sorry for yourself for one day. You've reached your maximum allotment.* Chase sipped the vodka, deciding it didn't taste too bad. The burn reminded him, for better or worse, that he was alive.

Toby's funeral had been today.

Chase closed his eyes, letting his head loll back on the couch cushions. The day swept by in his mind's eye, grim images he'd never imagined having to endure so soon, if ever. The gathering in the morning at the funeral home so everyone could watch, one final time, the video of photographs of Toby's life from birth up to a shot of him on a hike up to Mt. Rainier, taken late last spring, when the wildflowers were in glorious bloom, the snow-capped mountain peaks behind them. There was even a selfie of them on the gondola as they descended the mountain.

All the images in the video were accompanied by the plaintive words and music of Green Day, singing their signature song, ironically called "Good Riddance." Chase had been shocked when he heard the song title for the tribute. But Toby's sister, Elaine, had chosen the song for its reference to unpredictability, and the hopes for having "the time of your life." A tear dribbled down Chase's cheek as he recalled the strings and simple voice of the singer. He would never hear the song in the same way again. Right now, he didn't know if he could *bear* to hear it.

He had taken a copy of the DVD from Toby's family but buried it deep in one of his desk drawers when he got home. He didn't know when, if ever, he'd be able to bear watching it again. For now, it was torture and not comfort. He couldn't imagine a time when he would be composed enough to watch it without feeling extreme heartache and longing, impelled to tears and throat-burning sobs.

He hoped the day would arrive somewhere in the distant future, when watching the video would bring a smile to his face instead of tears to his eyes.

Better to leave the memories of his love in his mind, where Chase was certain they would remain forever, the horror of Toby's end gradually usurped by the passage of time and only good memories.

It would happen, Chase knew. The eventuality, though, was hard to believe at the moment.

He continued to survey the day.

The funeral, held in a Catholic church in Wallingford, was a standing-room-only affair, even though Toby had long ago left the church his family still clung to. "I'm not welcome in a Catholic church," Toby had said on more than one occasion. "But, oh, how I miss the rituals, the prayers, the holy water, and incense."

Chase sucked in a quivering breath as he recalled how many people had turned out—coworkers, friends, family that had flown out from Toby's home town, Wheaton, Illinois, to mark the passing of this once vibrant young man. He flashed quickly on the gunmetal gray coffin at the front of the church, topped with white lilies and greenery, and forced his mind away. Toby wasn't *really* in there. It was only his shell, a body, a collection of muscle, organs, tissue, and bones.

*It wasn't my Toby in that box.*

The graveside service was strange. He stood there amid the dark-garbed mourners, with their whispers, sniffling, and muffled sobs, in bright sunlight. Here they were in Seattle, known for its gray skies and drizzle, and the day was as bright, sunny, and perfect as one could imagine. Clear blue skies, unmarked by the presence of even one cloud. The temperature had risen into the low sixties, a record high for March.

It felt like a more fitting day for a picnic than a funeral, and Chase had wondered why the universe hadn't bowed its head to its great loss. Life, persistent and relentless, always moved on, regardless of how badly we hurt.

There had been a wake afterward at a restaurant on 45th Street in Wallingford, fittingly a Thai place that had been one of Toby's favorites. How he would have loved seeing everyone gathered, laughing, talking, and remembering him. He would have devoured the chicken satay, the green papaya salad, and the Pad Thai, wrapped in banana leaves. Chase hadn't been able to eat a thing, remembering the Thai buffet he had had catered for Toby's birthday, recalling how he and Mike had thrown all that food into the trash when they got home from the hospital that horrible night. It seemed a shame to waste so much good food, but Chase couldn't bear the thought of eating it—with its new connection to tragedy.

Actually, Chase didn't know if he could ever eat Thai again. But, he thought, smiling, Toby would have appreciated seeing his friends and family at the wake. If he was close by, he probably guided them in their choices.

Chase drained the glass and set it on the coffee table.

What now? It wasn't late, although it was full dark outside. He supposed he should try to eat something, but the idea of food remained repellant.

Even though it was only a little past nine, Chase thought there was really nothing left for him to do but strip out of his dark suit and crawl into bed, hoping the embrace of down and linen would deliver him into the oblivion of sleep.

He stood, loosened his tie and pulled it from his neck, letting it drop to the floor. He started toward the bedroom, dropping clothes as he went. He would pick them up in the morning. It would give him something to do.

In the bedroom, he stood naked in the doorway, waiting. He remembered so many nights when he had done something similar, stripped down to surprise Toby, already in bed. Chase could remember Toby's sleepy smile as he looked up at him, how just that slow, sexy grin could make him hard before he even crossed the room to join him on the bed. He sucked in a sob as a vision of outstretched arms rose up in his mind, torture and comfort in one package.

Chase was shocked to find himself growing aroused. He looked down at his dick, moving to an upright position with slow, jerky motions, as if it had a mind of its own.

*This is completely inappropriate*, he told his misbehaving member. *I'm supposed to be grieving.*

But his dick wouldn't listen, and so Chase walked awkwardly to the bed, his erection pointing out in front of him, and lay down across its surface.

When he shut his eyes, he swore he could feel Toby beside him.

Chase held his eyes closed and there it was, the feel of Toby's fingers, tracing a line across his chest, pausing to tweak each nipple, to roll them into hardness between thumb and forefinger. Chase shuddered. The hand massaged his pecs and Chase sighed as he felt Toby's warm breath on the hollow of his neck. Toby's hand moved downward, rubbing Chase's belly and playing with the line of coarse hair that trailed down into his pubes. Chase gasped as Toby's hand wrapped around his cock and squeezed, then loosened the pressure to move lazily up and down the length of his shaft, pausing every so often to finger his balls and the sensitive area behind them. Toby always did know just the right way to touch him, to make him shiver, to cause him to need and want more, to drive him to heights of pleasure, to tantalize him, to tease…

Toby's mouth found Chase's. He parted Chase's lips with his tongue and explored the inside of Chase's mouth, leaving behind a taste of cinnamon, and something indescribable that Chase could only think of as Toby's essence. Chase arched his back, pressing his body close to Toby's, so that they were aligned as one, muscle and skin intertwined in silken electricity. He grabbed the back of Toby's neck, forcing his face closer to his own, grinding his mouth hungrily against Toby's, their tongues dueling.

Toby pushed him down on the bed, using the weight of his body to do it, and instinctively Chase parted his legs, wrapping them first around his lover's thighs, then moving them up slowly, building the suspense, until at last his ankles rested on Toby's broad shoulders.

He bit his lip as Toby penetrated him, felt the little sting of pain as Toby passed through the taut ring of muscle guarding his ass, then relaxed into the deliciously full feeling of his man inside him.

*Home.*

Slowly, as if they were born to it, the pair began to move in perfect synchronicity. Chase removed his lips from Toby's so he could sigh and moan at the perfect feeling of Toby thrusting inside him, his cries of pleasure increasing right along with Toby's tempo as together they built to a perfect climax, one so strong Chase felt it not only in his cock and balls, but in his gut, the base of his spine. A climax so powerful it left him shuddering and laughing.

He opened his eyes to an empty room and a line of come liquefying across his stomach and chest. Chase swore he could hear the echo of Toby's voice, barely above a whisper.

"I love you."

Pale light lay across Chase's nude body in slats from the streetlight outside. "I love you too, sweetheart," he said into the room's shadows, searching it in vain for some sign of Toby.

He rolled gingerly to his side to grab some Kleenex and began cleaning himself up.

# Chapter Five

May in Seattle wasn't much different from January or February. The skies remained gunmetal gray, full of ominous clouds. The nights were still chilly, but the temperature rarely dipped low enough to be freezing, and a perpetual drizzle had settled across the city. The Cascades and Olympic ranges were hidden behind clouds of moisture, and Chase wondered if he'd ever see their glorious snow-capped heights again. The chill was the kind that seeped into one's very bones. No matter how much fleece, wool, or layers one donned, it seemed as though one could never get warm.

Chase trudged up the stairs to his empty condo.

Two months had passed since a drunk driver had killed his Toby in front of their home. Toby had just been crossing the street after getting off his bus, intent on getting home to spend his birthday with Chase.

The drunk driver had been intent on getting to the next happy hour.

It seemed like Toby had been gone forever. It seemed like he had passed only yesterday.

Sometimes, his presence in death loomed larger than it had in life. And Chase wasn't sure whether to be grateful for the fact or resentful of it.

Outside his front door, Chase slipped out of his wet shoes, placing them side by side on the little rubberized mat. He shook out his umbrella and put it in the stand. Then he put his key in the lock.

This routine, coming home from his job at a veterinary clinic where he answered phones, filed, and greeted clients and patients, hadn't varied since Toby's funeral. The sameness of it was somehow comforting, and yet at the same time underscored the emptiness he now felt each time he walked in the door.

There were times when he still expected to hear music coming from the kitchen—Donna Summer, Cyndi Lauper, or The B-52s—and to find Toby moving from counter to stove, where pots bubbled and pans sizzled with onions and garlic in a mix of butter and olive oil.

Those times when he simply forgot were the worst. The realization that he would never come back to such homespun comforts again could sometimes take his breath away with pain.

Tonight, he had no such illusions. The evening stretched before him like a night with a boring friend, predictable, not stimulating. A Lean Cuisine nuked and accompanied by a bottle of beer in front of the TV. Maybe he'd find something new to stream on Hulu or Netflix? Maybe, if he felt a little energy, he would slip into his Asics and take a jog around the neighborhood. More likely, he would simply drink another beer and fall asleep in front of the TV.

And then he would drop into bed, hoping he'd dream of Toby. But even though he was snoring and drooling on the couch, it would always take him hours to fall into that same comfortable slumber he experienced on the couch.

Why was life so cruel?

Dreams of Toby had only come twice, but he woke up feeling so happy, thrilled to have had just a few more minutes with him. He treasured those dreams so much he wrote them down on Post-it notes and kept them in one of his dresser drawers. He could look at them and the dream images would come back, broken, fragmented. But their essence remained—the togetherness one more time with Toby. But the sad thing was, after a while, even the dream images he'd written down wandered away, irretrievable. Even reading about them became like reading about someone else's memories, as if Chase hadn't been there.

He didn't dream of Toby nearly often enough. He wished there were a way he could force them. He wished he'd dream of him every night, every morning.

After changing into sweats and a long-sleeved Rat City Rollergirls T-shirt, Chase was just about to go into the kitchen to start his dinner when his cell phone, on the dining room table, chirped.

It had been so long since someone had called him that the ring sounded odd, foreign in the condo. But at least it was a small variation on the same old night he lived out over and over again.

He hurried to check out the display.

Mike.

It had been a while since he had heard from him. In the first week or two after Toby's funeral, Mike had called him every day, just to see how he was doing, to make small talk. But life interceded and the calls had become spaced further and further apart.

Chase understood. Mike couldn't babysit him forever.

He hit Accept and expected this to be, once again, Mike doing his duty to make sure Chase was okay, that he wasn't contemplating joining Toby in the great beyond.

At first, the call was just as he predicted. General inquiries about health, the weather, Chase's and then Mike's jobs—was the loss getting any easier to bear?

Chase blew out a sigh at that one. Easier? It was hard to say. Would it ever get easier? Chase's inclination was to simply be upbeat for Mike. After all, did the poor guy really care that much? Did he really want to hear how he hugged Toby's pillow at night? How he often found himself waking up mornings, completely forgetting that Toby had died and expecting, for a few brief, ignorant moments, to hear the shower running in the bathroom, or smell coffee brewing in the kitchen, or—worst of all—to find Toby lying next to him? As good a friend as he was, Mike was probably getting weary of hearing about such things, and so Chase said, "Yeah, it gets a little easier as time passes. But there will always be a scar. I don't know that I'll ever completely get over it."

"Of course you won't," Mike said softly. "Neither will I. Toby was a great man with a lot of heart and—funny. I miss him too, Chase."

Chase paced the condo, wondering if it was time to wrap up this conversation. But then Mike said something that piqued his interest.

"Hey buddy, I have a proposition for you."

Chase laughed. "You dirty man! You were Toby's best friend; how could you even think of such a thing?"

Mike chuckled. "I wasn't going to ask *that*, although I'd be lying if I said I'd never been tempted." Mike went quiet for a moment. "Sorry. But I did want to ask what you were doing for Memorial Day."

"Oh gee, I don't know, my dance card is so full." Chase loaded up his voice with sarcasm as he thought of the empty holiday weekend stretching before him at the end of the month. Toby had always been the one who set their social calendar, even if he was more truly the introvert—an introvert who had a long list of friends who were always calling and had now fallen silent. Chase would probably use the time to make an effort to chase away some of the dust and clutter that had accumulated over the past couple months, chores he simply hadn't the energy or motivation to tackle.

"Well, I was thinking you could come out to Chicago. It's been ages since you've been here. You haven't even seen my 'new' place, and it's two years old now." Mike had bought a condo in an old vintage building near the shores of Lake Michigan in the Edgewater neighborhood. Chase had seen a few pics of the place on Facebook, and it looked how he remembered Chicago apartments—with crown molding, built-in bookshelves on either side of a white-painted fireplace and touches like stained glass in the living room. It all seemed a world away.

"You're right about that. How is the place?" Chase felt a little twinge of anxiety pass through him. He didn't know if he could go back to Chicago without Toby. It was where the two of them had met, where their love had sparked and ignited, where they had shared so many happy, angry, sad, sexy, and glorious days and nights together.

Would going back without Toby be akin to ripping the scab off a wound? Would it harm him more than help him?

"It's good, a money pit, but good. I just had to have the whole place rewired. But you should see what I've done with the kitchen—glass tile, recessed lighting, retro mint-green Smeg appliances. It's cool."

"It sounds beautiful. You always did have such good taste. I've seen your pics on Facebook."

"Really? You never commented or liked anything, you lurker." Mike took a breath. "You're dodging me."

"Huh?"

"You know what I'm talking about. When I asked you to come out and visit, you didn't rush and say something like 'What a great idea!' or 'I'm busy then.' You changed the subject. But I'm not going to let you slip away that easy, buddy. Why don't you come out? I miss you."

"I miss you too, Mike. I just don't know..." His voice trailed off. Could he really explain his reluctance? Did he even want to try?

"You do remember, don't you, what happens in Chicago on Memorial Day Weekend?"

For a minute or two, Chase didn't. Backyard barbecues? The inaugural trip of the season to Hollywood Beach, Chicago's gay beach? Visiting Rosehill Cemetery?

And then it dawned on him. He chuckled, a low, throaty laugh that even to Chase's own ears sounded a little, well, dirty.

Mike joined in. "I knew you'd remember."

"International Mr. Leather," Chase said. "The leather high holidays."

"It's been years since you've been, man. Remember what fun we used to have when it was at the Congress Hotel and the three of us would descend on it together?"

"God, yes." Chase could remember; how could he forget? The International Mr. Leather competition had been held in Chicago since it began, back in 1979. IML was probably the biggest, most well-attended, and wildest gay leather event in the world. Every year, leather men (and some leather women) from all over the planet would descend upon a downtown hotel, taking it over for a weekend of wild partying, contests (Mr. IML, best bootblack), and no-holds-barred sex. The aroma and electricity of it wafted over every aspect of the weekend, including the huge leather mart, where one could sample the latest in erotic DVDs, whips, bondage paraphernalia, purple wands, chaps, vests, latex jock straps, and so much more. Never was there more man flesh and muscles on display than in the hosting hotel for IML, and all of it was sheathed, often indiscreetly, in leather, latex, and rubber.

It was hot. Parties, hookups, and orgies went on all weekend long, spilling over to Chicago's many bars and bathhouses.

Before they moved to Seattle, Toby and Chase had made it a tradition to go to IML together every year. Mike would often book a room, though he seldom got much sleep, and the three of them would terrorize the crowds of leather, rubber, and latex-clad men. Mike hooked up again and again, in rooms, bathrooms, stairwells, even once in the bushes beside bustling Wacker Drive. Mike was a libertine, or a slut for those more crudely inclined, but this truth was never more evident than IML weekend.

Toby and Chase enjoyed Mike's tomcat ways vicariously, and just the sight of so many gorgeous leather men all packed into one space inspired several consecutive nights of overheated passion between the two men.

Other things happened as well, but Mike was reeling him back to reality. "I can tell by your silence you have fond memories of IML." They both laughed.

"Yeah, I do," Chase admitted.

"We had some wild times, didn't we?"

"Well, you more than us, but yeah, I'd forgotten how much fun IML could be."

"Oh, I seem to remember you telling me about a time or two before you met Toby, when you attended IML as a bachelor, and you weren't as virtuous as you'd like to pretend." Mike laughed. "Don't forget who you're talking to here."

Chase remembered being a skinny twenty-something and going to his first IML with his best friend at the time, a journalist from one of the gay papers who was known for his handlebar moustache, his British accent, and his absolute lack of propriety or inhibition. "I know. I spilled all with you, Mike. And you promised to lock it away in the vault." His friend had pimped him out to an editor of some porno magazine—was it *Drummer*?—and Chase had ended up in a room with him, getting his ass eaten out for what seemed like hours.

"So you'll come?"

"I didn't say that."

"Oh come on. What's stopping you? Surely the animal hospital can get by without you for a few days, right? Fluffy's toenail trim can wait, or be supervised by someone else?"

"Hey, don't make fun of my work. It's important to me. But I don't know." Chase paused, debating whether he should tell Mike the real reason for his hesitation. Chase was tired of being the sad sack, the object of pity and sympathy. But then, what other excuse could he offer? Chase was a terrible liar, and to say he had other plans or had agreed to work the holiday shift for a coworker, an idea he now wished he'd thought of, wouldn't have come out anywhere near believable. No, he was stuck with the truth, and if it made Mike roll his eyes or feel sorry for him, or both, so be it. He took a breath and said, "I'm just afraid if I came back to town, it would be like reopening a wound. I mean, everywhere I'd go, there'd be memories of Toby."

"Yeah? So what? They're mostly good memories, right? So you revel in 'em. Embrace them. That's what I do. Toby was good for you, man. He was the best boyfriend a guy could want; I wish I could find someone like him. And you had a wonderful life, a great love together. So you treasure that. And bless those places that remind you of him."

"You're right."

"So you'll come. I've already looked into flights, and we can get you here pretty cheap if you book right now. The prices are going up every day—holiday weekend, you know. And you can stay with me." Chase could practically see Mike's leer through the phone. "I doubt very much I'll be crashing at home much that weekend anyway." Mike snickered. "So make an old friend happy. Say you'll come."

Chase paced the condo, unsure of what to say. Part of him wanted to go. Another part felt it would be a betrayal to Toby's memory to go without him. And how stupid was that? But emotions and logical thought didn't always go hand in hand. Yet another part maintained that to go would only make him feel worse. But then, Mike had a point about celebrating Toby's memories, rather than running from them.

Chase just didn't know if he was quite ready yet for celebration, or any of the other things a weekend in Chicago and at IML might promise. "I'll think about it," Chase finally said.

"Buddy, I hate to let you off the line without a commitment from you." Mike sounded serious and he went silent for several moments. "Would it help if I bought your ticket? Is money a problem?"

It was true Chase only made sixteen dollars an hour at the clinic, not exactly a rich guy's wages, but he had savings and even some money left from Toby's life insurance. He couldn't use funds as an excuse to get out of going, and he certainly wasn't so cheap that he'd take advantage of Mike. "No, I'm cool. The green is there."

"Then come. Say you'll get on a plane. Please."

Suddenly, it seemed like too much pressure. Chase snapped, literally and figuratively. "I said I need to think about it. And that's what I'm gonna do, okay? Listen, I have something on the stove I need to attend to, or it's gonna burn." He waited for Mike to say something, knowing he had stunned his friend with his sharp tone and already regretting it. "I'll call you. Okay?"

"Okay."

Chase hung up before Mike could try another line of persuasion. That was, even if the guy wanted to, after the way Chase had spoken to him.

The last thing he'd wanted to do was alienate Mike.

Chase went into the living room and sat on the couch, suddenly feeling too tired to make dinner and not hungry anymore anyway. He did a quick search on his iPad for *International Mr. Leather*. A blog came up near the top of the many listings and Chase recognized it as a blog Toby used to love, *Tales from the Sexual Underground*. Toby had an acquaintance who wrote it and was always telling him about new columns or reading to Chase from it. Yet, Chase had never been inclined to read the blog himself. This one, about IML, had been published several years ago, but must have been read a lot because of its high placement in the search rankings. It piqued his interest. He clicked on the blue link and started reading.

# "Gang Banged at International Mr. Leather"

Every May, they descend upon Chicago: the hungry, the sexually adventurous, the curiously twisted, the leather-clad. Yes, I'm talking about the International Mr. Leather Competition, the Windy City's nod to the kinky and the fetishistic.

One year, a group of horny, hearty sexual adventurers embarked eastward from San Francisco to Chicago's own IML with a purpose in mind, which was to not only engage in a cum-infested gang bang orgy, but to record that orgy on disc for posterity and profit. Treasure Island Media, a bareback video production company, headed up by the very friendly and very blood-engorged Mr. Paul Morris (along with his erstwhile sidekick, Mr. Damon Dogg), had the...um...tools at hand to produce one of the hottest male videos ever to emerge from the confines of the Windy City: *Riding Billy Wild, A Cum-Junkie's Gang Bang in Chicago.*

The seed, if you will, for this video, came from Mr. Wild himself, a hirsute, lean, and handsome slut puppy from the City by the Bay, who offered to pay to have Treasure Island Media record his adventures. Quicker than you can say, "I'm cummin' up your ass!" cameras were in place, and a long line of known and unknown quantities were queuing up for a crack at Billy's crack.

The result is a film that is almost relentless in its depiction of male-to-male bareback action (this article, by the way, is not about the pros or cons of gay bareback sex; we're all big boys and know the risks...). I watched it with eyes glazed over and a tightness in my nether regions that just wouldn't go away. I lost count of the scores of men who took control of Billy's ass and mouth, one after the other. Heavens! What does one do for an encore? Local men (such as Lee Clifford), unknown men, men who didn't want their faces shown, and sexual superstars such as Matt Sizemore and Will West all "came" together to make an explosive record of an insatiable bottom's attempts to get sated. Those looking for a story or a moral in Riding Billy Wild will be disappointed.

The last scene in *Riding Billy Wild*, however, has nothing to do with Billy and everything to do with Treasure Island Media's own Damon Dogg's visit to a local—and raunchy—leather watering hole. Thanks to the magic of night vision technology, we get to see Mr. Dogg on his knees in the backroom, begging for cum...he even offers to buy the owner of one large organ a shot for a shot, if you get my drift.

All in all, the men from San Francisco (and the ones here, too) came away from the experience satisfied. You can satisfy yourself vicariously when you order the film from Treasure Island Media (www.treasureislandmedia.com).

Now, let's hear all about the experience from the owner of Treasure Island Media, Paul Morris, whom I was lucky enough to catch up with between takes. Here's what he had to say:

TSU: What made you decide to film Billy Wild?

PM: The first time I met Billy I knew I wanted to film him. It's usually a very quick thing for me; I can tell if a guy is coming in because he thinks he's a pornstar (whatever that may be), because he needs cash, or because he's a true and driven sexaholic. It's the guys who live for sex that I'm really interested in, being one myself. Obsession loves company.

TSU: How did you decide to hook up?

PM: Billy wrote to me offering to pay me if he could do a scene with a bunch of guys. That's probably the best way to get my attention; it really tells you something about a guy. He came over to my place to talk about possibilities and as soon as he walked in I knew I wanted to work with him. His physical look is so All-American and wholesome and is such a great frame for the immense libidinal heat that he radiates.

TSU: What else about Billy appealed to you?

PM: I'm obsessed with men of all types; I have the most promiscuous eye in the world. But when I meet someone like Billy I can't wait to throw him into action, to see how he reacts to the men I surround him with. I learn from people like that; I get re-inspired. I couldn't wait to see Billy's eyes as he got fucked by a room full of men he'd never met.

TSU: How did you solicit participants?

PM: We put a notice up on our website, but the rest was pretty much word of mouth. Our guys, Damon Dogg and Jesse, wandered around IML and if they saw a guy who looked like he might fit into a bareback gangbang orgy, they'd approach him. Sometimes it worked out, sometimes it didn't. At one point they put a collar around Billy's neck and led him around bareass, telling guys that they could fuck him if they showed up for the gangbang.

RR: Anything unusual happen during the, um, shooting? Funny? Disastrous?

PM: Well, the room got so crowded that the line of men waiting to get in stretched all the way down the hall. That meant that the door to the room was basically open throughout the orgy, which got some raised eyebrows from the hotel staff. And once they got in some guys were a bit out of place. But even if they weren't into joining in and fucking Billy, the guys definitely enjoyed the voyeuristic aspect of the scene. I think everyone had a great time. Billy certainly enjoyed the attention...and all the cocks.

RR: So, who is Billy Wild?

PM: Billy has a regular job in San Francisco, wears a suit and a tie (and looks terrific in them), has a boyfriend (who is without doubt one of the most liberal and understanding men in the world), and is one of the nicest and most charming guys I've met. If you met him on the street, you'd have no idea that he had this profoundly slutty side to him.

TSU: How did you manage to get the scene at the _____ (a local bar)?

PM: I was surprised by that one. Damon Dogg loves to go out to bars, get shit-faced on shots of tequila and suck dick. He's known for that in SF, where he regularly sucks off everyone at the Hole in the Wall, or My Place, or the Powerhouse (the bartenders at the Powerhouse are apparently planning to buy him a personalized stool to give his knees a break). After finishing the Billy Wild shoot, Damon needed to blow off some steam, so he dragged our casting director, Nick, to _____. Nick always carries a small video camera with him in case he encounters someone interesting. He likes to tape them to see how they look on camera. Damon got drunk and started blowing guys and Nick just started to tape it. A couple of times the bartenders told Nick and Damon to cut it out, but once Damon gets started he's hard to stop. And apparently at least one of the bartenders is a fan of Damon's video series, "Damon Blows America". My favorite part of that "scene" is when you can hear Damon offering to buy guys shots if they'll feed him their load. He does that all the time in SF, which goes a long way toward explaining why Damon is always broke, but with a belly full of semen. The footage has a kind of eerie quality to it because the bar was dark and Nick used Night Vision.

TSU: What did you think of Chicago and IML?

PM: IML was fun. Everyone had a great time. What a beautiful and great city. And the people were incredibly nice. We're used to San Franciscans, who can be kind of cold and intense. The people we met in Chicago were warm, friendly, and universally great. And the men are over-the-top sexy.

TSU: Any future Chicago productions planned? Can I be in 'em (I laughed)?

PM: As a matter of fact, we loved Chicago so much that we're setting up a production office there. Brad McGuire, a great guy who happens to be sexy as hell (and sports one of the biggest and most beautiful uncut schlongs I've seen), is going to be in charge of it. We've already started shooting. I'm looking forward to spending a lot of time in Chicago, and I'm really looking forward to getting the sexy men of Chicago in front of our cameras...and that includes you!

When Chase finished reading, his face was hot. It literally felt as though what lay beneath his skin was on fire.

He laughed at himself. *You little prude*! The article brought back a lot of memories, though, maybe not as slutty as what he'd just read about, but his own experience nonetheless.

He set down his iPad and let his mind drift back...

# Chapter Six

May, sometime in the mid-1990s. The International Mr. Leather competition had been going full swing for over a decade, growing more and more each year until it had become the all-out international competition and event it was today, with contestants and revelers now taking over the ballroom and several floors of hotel rooms.

Chase's first IML took place at the Congress Hotel. The Congress was older, a bit south of the more refined part of Michigan Avenue, and showed its age, but not necessarily in a bad way. Like an older person who refused to resort to tricks like plastic surgery to look young, it had a kind of tired dignity—and elegance.

The touch of seediness the hotel had—at least back in those days—made it the perfect venue for the leather competition; the kink and fetish-absorbed participants for the weekend fit right in. Step inside the Congress during IML and one was transported to a different world, one that revolved around hirsute men in leather and latex and that smelled of animal hide, cigarette smoke, and poppers.

IML, back then, was not even on Chase's radar. He might have seen a mention of it in the *Windy City Times* or *Gay Chicago*, or one of the local leather bar ads promoting it, but he wouldn't have thought much of it. He would have shrugged and flipped the page of whatever gay rag he was reading. One wouldn't find Chase lounging back then at a place like the Eagle, or Touché, or the Double AA Meat Market. Frankly, those places with their rough-looking men in their chaps and harnesses scared the hell out of him. Intellectually, he was aware that these men were probably not much different from Chase on the inside, and that their bar talk probably revolved around the same things he heard at places like Sidetrack or Roscoe's, but their grizzled, tough-guy exteriors put him off.

And excited him.

But he would never admit that, not even to his closest friend.

So Chase greeted the phone call that came from his friend Vincent that Saturday morning in May with the same kind of mixed feelings he had experienced with Mike's invitation a few minutes ago. In his mind's eye, he could still see the boy/man he was back then, a cordless phone held to his ear.

"What are you up to today?" Vincent never failed to get to the point right off the bat. His cigarette-scarred, British-accented voice came through the phone, making Chase want to giggle and then, perhaps, shower.

Chase remembered the old studio apartment he lived in back then, at the lake end of Jarvis Avenue in Rogers Park. It was tiny, all one room, save for the black-and-white tiled bath with its clawfoot tub, but oh how he'd loved that place. What it lacked in size, it made up for in convenience (step out the door and he was on the beach; walk a couple blocks to the west and he was at the L station and could travel just about anywhere he desired in the city from that starting point). It also had amazing views of Lake Michigan and Chase never tired of the big ocean-like body of water's changing moods—it could be aqua and tropical appearing one day, shimmering in the sun, and gray and foreboding the next, with surging waves crashing against the boulders at the edge of the beach.

That particular Saturday morning, Chase had just gotten up and was imagining the bliss of simply drinking coffee and peering out at the day, the Tempo section of the *Tribune* spread out before him. He'd have the new Philip Glass album he'd just picked up at Tower Records on his stereo. Maybe he'd soft boil a couple of eggs, make some toast with lots of butter.

He recalled the day being gray and chilly, his windows rain smeared.

He responded to Vincent with, "Not much. I have to go to Jewel and get some food. The cupboards are pretty bare."

Vincent made a tsk sound and announced, "That's not what you're doing today."

Vincent coughed out his version of a laugh, and Chase knew, whatever the older man had in mind, there would be no refusing him. And why would he want to, anyway? Whatever Vincent had planned had to be better than sniffing melons and examining packages of stew meat at the Jewel in Evanston. Vincent was always good for a laugh and irrepressible when it came to finding, and reveling in, mischief.

"Okay, I give up, Vincent. So clue me in—what am I doing today?"

"You're coming to IML with me."

Chase snorted. "IML? My dear, I don't have a thing to wear to such an affair. Besides, why would you want to go there today? Aren't most of the leather guys sleeping, waiting to come out after dark, like vampires?"

"Oh, you *are* the clueless little homo, aren't you? There's a huge leather mart going all day—whips and chains, bondage furniture, porn, leather gear. And tons of hot leather men, all cruising around the stalls, looking for someone to corrupt." Vincent chuckled.

Chase knew he was the corruptee Vincent had in mind.

"Besides, I need to cover it for the paper." Vincent was one of the few, if not the only, full-time reporter for the *Windy City Times* and went to every gay event he could cram into his calendar, usually returning home to his long-suffering partner stinking drunk with a little cocaine powder under his nostrils. Amazingly, his writing was always witty, concise, fact-checked, and above reproach.

"Okay, but I still don't know what to wear."

"Sweetie, just take one of your flannel shirts and cut the sleeves off; do the same with the legs of a pair of old jeans. Grab a pair of boots, construction or combat, and you'll fit right in. Got a wife beater?"

"Yeah." Chase imagined himself in the ensemble Vincent described, and felt heat rise to his cheeks. He couldn't imagine going out dressed like that, especially not parading down the street and riding the L downtown in it. He could just imagine the looks he'd have to endure.

But he went ahead and followed his friend's advice. He even found an old dog tag, promo for one of the bars, in his sock drawer. After getting off the L at Wilson to make the trip to Vincent's apartment, he deluded himself into thinking maybe folks would simply mistake him for a construction worker on his way to a site. That illusion shattered like glass when a carload of teenage boys roared by on Irving Park Road. One of them shouted, "Faggot!"

as the driver of the Monte Carlo hit the gas, too cowardly to pause to see Chase's stunned expression.

Chase quickened his pace to Vincent's apartment, located appropriately enough on a street called Bittersweet.

Vincent waited in the hallway for Chase as the elevator doors for his floor opened. He wore a black gauzy shirt, tight black jeans with a studded belt, and combat boots. But what really took Chase's breath away was Vincent's face. Vincent had always had piercings, not only in his nose and left ear, but now he had joined the two with a sterling silver chain. He had waxed his salt and pepper mustache so that it stood straight out on either side of his face. Chase was certain it was one of the few mustaches that could actually be seen from behind.

"Look at you," Chase gasped.

"Face done up like a Christmas tree, right?" Vincent laughed and brought out a whip and tried unsuccessfully to crack it. "Uh, we'll just leave this at home." He hurried back to his apartment, flung the whip inside, and came back.

"Ready for your first IML?" He took Chase's arm, leading him back to the elevator.

Chase had no answer for that. He most decidedly was *not* ready, nor did he think he would ever be. To be honest, he was a little apprehensive about hanging out with the leather crowd. They seemed intimidating.

He began to relax as they headed downtown on the L. Leather, apparently, loved company!

It was reassuring to see he and Vincent weren't the only ones headed south for the leather extravaganza. Their car alone was half full of leather people, mostly men, but there were some fierce-looking women too. It was surreal to see on this bright spring afternoon.

When they got to the Congress and entered the huge leather mart, Chase was almost breathless. Heat rose to his face and stayed there the better part of the day. He could only hope it made him look more fetching—a bloom of vitality, or something like that.

The ballroom where the leather mart was set up rose two stories high. Every inch had been crammed with booths selling things you'd never find at your local Target or Walmart. There was everything from gay porn (from mild to wild, as they say), to whips, to purple wands (people actually enjoyed being electrocuted? It was a revelation to Chase), to dildos in all different lengths, widths and colors, to leather vests, harnesses, chaps and more, to bondage chains and ropes, to body jewelry, to stuff beyond Chase's wildest imaginings. Was this a dream? The leather mart was like Costco for the polymorphously perverse.

There were bondage demonstrations going on. Chase paused to watch a man who was being mummified in duct tape.

A sign directed passersby to room 338, where a fisting demonstration would be given at 2:00 p.m. Chase laughed and wondered what kind of refreshments would be served at such a demonstration—and would there be hand sanitizer? He didn't know if he could bear to watch someone's arm disappearing into a slack and willing hole. He broke out in giggles as he wondered how many wristwatches could get lost in the process.

And would such a loss be covered by one's homeowners insurance? He could just imagine filing *that* claim.

Chase paused to watch a young skinhead, clad only in a leather jockstrap and harness, get tied to a St. Andrew's cross, his green eyes lit up with pleasure. A red ball gag adorned his mouth, so you couldn't hear his giggles, or sighs, or moans, as a heavily tattooed man in a leather skirt passed a feather over his skinny body.

Slaves were being led around on leashes by their masters, topless women, men wearing chaps and jockstraps, their asses bare, hardcore gay videos being played on monitors, a guy getting his dick pierced while an excited crowd gathered around to watch. When he'd taken a break to piss, there was at least one sexual act already heatedly taking place in a stall a few feet over.

The guy next to him had nodded toward Chase's stream of piss. "I'll take that if you want, sir."

Chase felt heat rise to his face yet again and hurried from the men's room without taking the time to wash his hands or even glance back at the generous watersports aficionado.

Chase felt like he'd landed on some fetishy alien planet.

*My God, Michigan Avenue and normal life are really only a few yards away. What would some of the people in those cars outside think of what was going on in here?*

Chase couldn't imagine.

"So what do you think, sweetie?" Vincent asked. "Feeling right at home? Want to run right out and get yourself a collar? Studded arm band—for your left arm, if I'm guessing right? Maybe get your taint pierced?" Vincent chuckled, raising his eyebrows.

"Unbelievable," was all Chase was able to mutter.

He knew such a world existed—he'd passed by the leather bars and seen contingents of leather folk at the pride parade and Halsted Market Days in the summer. But he'd never gotten this close. In his heart of hearts, he had to admit that he was equal parts aroused and repelled. He figured the latter part was powered by good old Catholic guilt. He'd be lying if he said the scene didn't excite him. He'd never thought of himself as the leather type, but he had to admit being in this crush of very manly looking men all clad in different iterations of the leather and Levi theme had set his heart to pounding and his dick to twitching.

Chase reeled himself back to the present, alone in his Seattle apartment, and smiled at the memory of his debut at IML. He recalled how his fascination with all the hot men there was a surprising and delightful two-way street.

He couldn't believe he was getting checked out, and so often! Heads swiveled in neck-wrenching turns as he walked by. He heard "Woof" uttered softly more than once as he passed a man or group of men. Three guys stopped him to ask if they could take his picture.

Chase's grin broadened as he remembered another striking image from that day—this one also connected to photography. Somehow, a photographer from one of the gay magazines covering the event coerced him into letting him take a picture of Chase in one of the service stairwells. Well, maybe coerced wasn't the right word—the photographer had led a very willing Chase to the stairwell and even got him to open the button fly on his cut-off Levi's. Chase had been so excited by the attention and the onlookers peering in through the service door that he sported a raging hard-on. He was both embarrassed and proud of it.

And the photographer's camera simply went *click, click, click.*

Chase wondered where the photos had ended up, who had seen it.

The climax, in more ways than one, of his IML first-time memories, came when he and Vincent were cruising the upstairs retail stalls. They stopped at a booth for a very hardcore gay SM magazine out of San Francisco that today Chase could not even recall the name of. They flipped through several magazines on the display table, chuckling and growing silent at graphic pictures of muscular naked men in some very compromising, and very arousing, positions.

Even with all this naked photographic flesh on display, Chase couldn't help drawing his gaze away from the magazine pages to the guy manning the booth. They later found out he was the editor of the magazine. He was tall, with reddish brown hair, a goatee, and dark-blue eyes underneath lashes too long for a man. Where the goatee did not reach, there was a pale smattering of red stubble. The guy wore a simple olive-drab T-shirt, faded jeans, and a leather bar vest.

Chase was in love, or more properly, in lust.

The guy smiled at him, and Chase's knees went weak.

As they were walking away from the booth, Vincent asked, "You like that?"

Chase had thought it would be useless to pretend he didn't know what, or whom, Vincent was talking about. Hell, Chase's eyes were just about rolling out of his head, along with his tongue.

He smiled meekly at Vincent. "Oh yeah. He's hot."

"Want me to get him for you?" Vincent grinned wickedly. "I'll be your pimp!"

Before Chase could say anything to stop him, or even reach out to grab his departing figure, Vincent was heading rapidly back to the booth. Chase watched helplessly as Vincent worked his charm on the redhead.

They leaned their heads close together conspiratorially. They both glanced over at Chase, smiling. Chase could feel his face redden and his heart rate spike. Why was Vincent doing this? Was he really trying to pimp Chase out to the magazine editor? Chase wasn't sure which he dreaded more: Vincent succeeding or not succeeding.

In less than five minutes, Vincent sauntered back over to Chase, wearing a cat-that-ate-the-canary grin. Chase glanced over his shoulder and saw the editor conferring with another guy in the booth.

"Well, sweetie, you're good to go."

"No!" Chase gasped. He looked over at the redhead once more and couldn't hold back the rush of lust that coursed through him, causing his dick to raise its purple head and stiffen in anticipation. It was almost as if the thing knew Chase's own thoughts before he did. "Really?"

"Really. Now get on over there. He's only been relieved from the booth for an hour. And I expect you both to come back from his room *relieved*." Vincent chuckled and pushed Chase toward the booth. "Go on, then. I'll want to hear all the sordid details afterward."

Chase had never dreamed when he left his apartment that morning his day would shape up like this, but for once, he forced himself to let go of his inhibitions and simply enjoy the good luck that had come his way.

Keith, as he told him his name was, waited for him by the booth. The two didn't say much as they took the elevator up to Keith's room. And really, what was there to say? They both knew what was about to happen, and the only mystery was who would do what to whom—and for how long. Somehow keeping details like that unsaid had its appeal for Chase.

Once inside the room, neither man wasted any time, especially Keith, who hailed from San Francisco and had a job that involved reading all day about sex, and looking at naked men. Keith was on his knees within five seconds of closing and locking the hotel room door, expertly unbuttoning Chase's shorts and tugging them down to his ankles.

Chase was expecting to feel Keith's mouth on his cock and his dick was already twitching and dripping precome in anticipation.

But he didn't get what he expected, not at first, anyway. Keith's hands pushed at his hips, turning Chase so he faced away from him. He sighed as he felt Keith's strong hands parting his ass cheeks, and then moaned out loud as Keith pressed his hot tongue to the crack of his ass, then burrowed it directly into the tight little pucker, nestled amid Chase's soft brown curls.

Soon, both men were making guttural animal sounds as Chase bent over to give Keith better access, and to continue to drive him upward in frenzied pleasure. Keith knew how to use his tongue to elicit an electric trail from Chase that went from his dick to his heart, then back again. Chase tried to keep his own hand off his dick and failed miserably, working it up and down, lubed with spit, as Keith devoured his ass.

He felt himself getting close to coming as Keith licked and burrowed into his ass, taking a minute out here and there to lap at his balls and to roughly, and almost painfully, yank his dick back between his thighs so he could suck the head of it and use the tip of his tongue to lap up the juices now flowing freely. The feel of his stubble against the silk of his ass cheeks was indescribable—rough and irritating, yet oh so *good*.

Chase's breathing quickened as he felt the approach of his orgasm. At the sound of Chase's panting, Keith suddenly stopped, reaching between Chase's legs to squeeze his dick hard at the base. "No. Not yet."

Keith pushed Chase roughly toward the bed, slamming him facedown into its unmade surface. Chase pulled a pillow under his head, then—brazenly—positioned the other pillow under his crotch, raising his ass in the air. Mutely, he watched as Keith at last stripped out of his clothes, revealing a thin, ripped body almost completely covered in reddish down. A long pole of a dick, with a purple vein snaking its way around the shaft, rose up from between his thighs. Keith fumbled in the nightstand drawer and pulled out a condom and a bottle of lube. Hurriedly, he rolled the condom onto his shaft and then slicked it up with the slippery stuff.

Chase closed his eyes, barely able to swallow in anticipation. He hadn't bottomed all that much, but Keith's tongue and his manly assertiveness had more than prepared him. He wasn't worried about pain. He was simply worried about Keith getting over here *fast* and covering Chase's body with his own—and sliding that perfect and beautiful dick all the way up inside him.

Chase had to wait for only about ten seconds for his wish to come true. Keith grabbed Chase's shoulders as he mounted him, spreading himself out on top of Chase like a big, furry blanket. He went slow at first, easing first the tip of his cock in gently, then adding a little more, inch by inch, until he was buried all the way inside Chase, his coarse pubic hair rough against his ass.

He moved slowly at first, making sure Chase was comfortable. Hell, Chase was beyond comfortable. He was in ecstasy. Gradually, Keith increased his tempo and pace until he was at last slamming hard into Chase's ass, pounding him into the pillow and making him cry out, but not with pain. Both men's cries permeated the dank little hotel room, until at last the thrusting, and Chase bucking his hips back against Keith to force him deeper inside, reached a crescendo and both men bellowed out their pleasure, exploding at the very same time.

Chase swore he could feel Keith's dick twitching in his ass.

As he gradually came back to reality and his breathing and heart rate returned to normal, Chase thought how the world had disappeared under Keith's magic tongue, hands, and dick, and only then did he wonder how Vincent was doing.

And how much time had passed.

He shook his head and brought himself back to the present. Rimming, that's what they called it. He brought out his phone, looked up Tales from the Sexual Underground and then used the search function on the blog to see if its author had written anything about the topic of, clinically-speaking, analingus.

Indeed, he had.

## "Fill it to the Rim"

Ask your mother, or any of your straight friends, to use the word "rim" in a sentence as a verb and they may be hard pressed to come up with a response. Oh sure, Mom might say, "Grandma's lovely mixing bowl was *rimmed* in *fleur-de-lis*." But for the most part, your straight friends probably think of the word rim as a noun.

But ask your gay brethren and you'll come up with an entirely different response. The rim of their favorite coffee cup is probably the last thing to come to their filthy little minds when that particular three-letter word arises in conversation. "Rimming" or "tossing a salad" are just a couple of metaphors for the act known less delicately as "eating butt" or for those of a more clinical semantic bent, analingus.

But how safe is putting your tongue where the sun don't shine? Once again, I will reiterate my claim, before I go any further, that I am not a doctor, nor have I ever even played one on TV, so what I say here should not be construed as medical advice. It's only the results of my own feeble research into the topic that I present here, so take it with a grain of salt...or a shot of penicillin...or a hepatitis vaccination. Which brings me to my first point: hepatitis. Other than winding up with a shit-eating grin, your biggest risk when it comes to rimming is contracting hepatitis, A or B, maybe even C. Face it, butt munchers, the easiest way to get hepatitis is through fecal matter, and you're bound to come into contact with some if you go sticking your nose (and your mouth) in a loved one's butthole, however tight, pink, hairy or beautiful that little rosebud may be. The good news here is that you can allay many of your worries by visiting your doctor and getting yourself vaccinated against the dreaded virus(es). Then you can munch away with abandon, bearing in mind that you have *not* been vaccinated against other nasty little critters you could pick up this way, like parasites. As with most any gestures of affection, you must weigh the risks and benefits of any such display and decide what is right for you. Keeping your nose out of others' business is your decision as an educated consumer.

You may be wondering about that old bugaboo we hear so much about these days: HIV. From what I've learned, rimming is not all that likely to give you the dreaded virus, provided you have a healthy mouth (no cuts, sores, blisters, icky gums, etc.) and he has a clean ass free from any sores, rips or cuts. We won't even get into *felching* here.

I guess when it comes to tossing a salad, cleaning the kitchen, or whatever fanciful term you choose to dress up your taste for butt with, the key words are common sense and caution.

So, dear ones, I close with two clichés: *bottoms up*! And *bon appetit*!

Chase shook his head, grinning at the blog and its wit. Oddly enough, he found himself suddenly famished, and that tickled him.

He got up, went into the kitchen and threw a Lean Cuisine into the microwave. For good measure, he found a heart of romaine in the fridge that was almost past its freshness date and broke it up in a bowl for a salad. For the first time in a long time he felt happy, lighter. In the long days and nights of grief following Toby's death, he had almost forgotten what it felt like to be young, uninhibited, and carefree. Lustful! Chase couldn't remember the last time he'd even beat off.

Life was out there; he had lost touch with it.

The memories brought him back, reminding him he was still a young man (youngish, anyway) and that Toby, most of all, wouldn't want him to spend the rest of what remained of his life mourning him.

Would he?

No, of course not. Chase leaned forward on the couch and snatched up his cell. Mike picked up on the first ring.

"So, were you serious about that invitation to Chicago—and IML?"

The relief and pleasure Chase heard coming through the line made him smile, again. "Yes! Yes, of course!"

"Well, I think it might be good to get away for a few days, see my old friend. Come back to the city I love."

"And see some hot men?"

"That too. That too." An odd sense that he was betraying Toby made his stomach twist. He tried to tell himself that he was being illogical, but the gut knows what it knows.

They talked only for a few minutes more, plotting out Chase's trip, which online booker would be best to go with, which day would be good for arrival, and which for departure. At first, Chase had thought he'd come in on Thursday night and leave Sunday morning.

"Come on, man," Mike said.

"What do you mean?"

"That isn't nearly enough time. You've been through a lot, Chase. Take a little vacation, relax a while. Three or four days with you is not gonna be enough, not for me and not for the guys at IML. Besides, the big ball at the end of the event is always Sunday night—you don't want to miss that, do you?"

"Okay, okay. I'll leave on Monday, then."

"Good Lord, I really do need to get you to loosen up! Listen, plan on a week, ten days if you can get away from work that long. I've got plenty of PTO, so I'll take the time off too. We'll have a blast. And you stay with me—cheap and easy. I was referring to myself, by the way, but the accommodations are those too."

Chase laughed, warming more and more to the idea.

He knew Mike was really not thinking so much about IML, or all the fun things the two of them could do in his hometown. He was being considerate of Chase, wanting him to make the transition from grieving widower to functioning member of society once more. "You know what, Mike?"

"Huh?"

"Thanks."

"Ah, it's nothin'. A long time ago, I promised Toby I would take care of you. So, buddy, this is just all in a day's work." Mike laughed.

"You're too good. And when did you promise Toby that? I've always been pretty good at taking care of myself, you know."

Mike was quiet for a moment. "No, it's true. When you guys first got together, Toby and I were out having a beer at Touché and I was trying to coax him into the backroom for a little anonymous sex and, for once, he wouldn't go. He told me he had met the only man he wanted to have sex with, anonymous or otherwise. He said there was no one in that backroom who could compare to you.

"*And* he told me you guys were gonna be together forever, even though you'd had, like, two dates. He asked me then to always watch out for you if anything ever happened to him." Mike paused. "Chase? It's true."

Chase tried to find his voice. Mike's words had done what he was sure the guy hadn't intended—made him cry. There was a big lump in his throat, and his eyes burned and itched with the hot flow of tears. "Damn it," he whispered.

"You okay?"

"Better than okay." Chase took a deep breath and pulled himself together. "I believe you." His voice cracked a little. "That sounds just like my Toby."

Chase's breath heaved once more, and he decided if this wasn't going to be some transcontinental sob fest he should end the call. "Listen, man, I need to get on the computer and book those tickets."

"Can't wait, Chase."

"Me neither."

"See you soon."

"Soon."

Chase hit the button to end the call.

# Chapter Seven

Chase was able to book a direct flight on Alaska Airlines to Chicago from Seattle. The round-trip ticket had cost him more than a week's pay, but Chase didn't want to bother with layovers, and the fact of the matter was, so close to a holiday weekend, all the airlines had jacked up their fares.

It had been a long time since he'd traveled anywhere—that's how he justified the cost. He tried to push from his mind the recollection that Toby and he had discussed taking a trip over to Kauai that summer. Chase had never been to Hawaii at all and Toby had only been once, but that was long enough to fall in love with what he, and others, referred to as the garden island because of how unspoiled it was.

Now, as the plane descended into O'Hare International Airport, Chase wasn't thinking about airfares, or whether he had spent too much. The pilot welcomed them to Chicago and told them that the weather outside was cloudy and the temperature was in the low sixties. Chase thought this sounded typical for Chicago, and remembered all the many Memorial Day weekends where it was chilly and rainy. It had happened so frequently, it had almost become a standing joke.

As the plane taxied to the gate, Chase wasn't sure how he was going to feel once he got off the plane.

Chicago had been home to him more than any other place on earth; he had lived in the Windy City for so many years and thought he would never leave it. But then Toby got the offer from Microsoft, and they found themselves winging their way across the country to the West Coast and a brand new life. Chase had never been to Seattle; indeed, he'd never even made it farther west than St. Louis, but he'd agreed to make the cross-country move to support Toby and his career. The Microsoft gig was a great thing. The last thing Chase wanted to do was stand in his man's way.

It didn't matter that Seattle was new, untested, unknown. He was with Toby, and the fact of the matter was home was wherever they were together—it had never been dependent on a physical space, something as insignificant as bricks and mortar.

Now that Toby was gone, Chase had wondered many times if he shouldn't just quit his job at the animal hospital and go back to Chicago. There was little holding him to Seattle. Plus there was the fact that he couldn't afford the rent on their beautiful Capitol Hill place. He'd either have to get a roommate, an idea he abhorred, or move. And where would he go?

But the one thing that had stopped him from seriously considering moving back, and the one thing he feared most right at this very moment, was that he wasn't sure how he'd cope with all the memories of Toby he knew would suddenly surround him. Oh sure, there were plenty of memories in Seattle as well, but the couple hadn't had long enough to put down the kind of roots they had in Chicago.

Everywhere in Chicago he'd find Toby's face, his essence, his—oh, it sounded so silly, even to his mind—his

"Tobiness." He'd find him at Millennium Park, reflected back in the giant metal sculpture, affectionately known as *the bean,* that tourists always crowded around taking pics of themselves reflected in its shiny chrome surface. He'd find him at Big Chick's, the only bar the pair of them frequented once they became a couple, with its friendly, laid-back crowd and its awesome art collection. He was sure to catch a glimpse of someone just like him walking along Hollywood Beach, where the two of them had spent many happy Sunday summer afternoons, sweating, coconut-scented flesh pressed arm to arm on an old sheet laid on the sand, trying to be discreet about ogling all the tan muscle on display around them. He'd see Toby's rapturous face across from him at Hai Yen, their favorite Vietnamese spot on Argyle Street, as Toby tucked into a plate of their sublime green papaya salad or their shrimp on skewers of sugar cane.

Chase wondered, as he stood to pull down his duffel from the overhead compartment and sling his backpack over one shoulder as he prepared to deplane, if he would be able to resist making a tour of the neighborhoods they had lived in over the years: Edgewater, Rogers Park, and Ravenswood.

Would looking at each building and peering up at the windows of their old homes arouse in him unbearable grief? At those windows, would he see ghosts of himself and Toby, their younger selves going about happy lives, ignorant of how little time they really had left together? Or would stopping by their old homes simply infuse him with warm memories? He didn't know.

If he simply remembered the happier times, would he doubt their ability to ever come into his life again?

The row of seats before him emptied, and Chase made his way down the close aisle in coach. His ears had yet to pop from the flight, so the sounds around him were muffled, leaving him feeling even more isolated and alone with his thoughts.

Mike had offered to pick him up at the airport. No, Mike had insisted on it. But Chase wouldn't allow it. He needed the time the trip to Mike's apartment would afford to pull himself together, to make sure, as his mother used to say, he was "presentable for company." Chase was an introvert through and through and knew that time by himself before seeing Mike would give him the energy he needed for their reunion. The last time he had seen him was after Toby's funeral.

He also just wanted to have a short while to touch the pain and pleasure of his life here with Toby. He knew a cab ride to Mike's apartment on Kenmore would take only a half hour or forty-five minutes, depending on traffic, but he opted for the cheaper, and infinitely longer, L ride from the airport to Mike's. The time on the train would allow him to ease back into the city, to see its people on first the blue line and then the red, to watch as apartment buildings and storefronts flew by, their lights coming on to ward off the darkness of the encroaching night.

He headed through the airport, dragging his bag along behind him, and followed the signs for the subway. When he got to the stairs leading onto the platform, he was happy to see a train in the station, waiting to take him downtown, where he would switch the blue line for the red at Roosevelt and then head north to Mike's stop at Bryn Mawr.

Once he boarded the train, Chase waited...and waited. The train didn't lurch into motion until about fifteen minutes had passed and the car had filled almost to capacity. It became more crowded at each subsequent stop it made along the Kennedy Expressway, Wicker Park, and finally, as it plunged into the downtown subway, people stood elbow to elbow in the aisles.

Chase was surprised that he didn't feel much. Wasn't that the way emotions always went though? You could never really predict how you would feel in a situation until you were in it. Chase assumed his memories would be flying by like a movie projected at high speed, but once the train got going, its rhythmic motion lulled him into a state of relaxation. He stared out the windows at the familiar sights of the city, at the traffic rushing by with a sense of, if anything, homecoming. He barely noticed the train getting emptier at each stop.

It felt right to be here.

He opened his phone and scanned it to pass the time. He was now a confirmed fan, one of thousands, of Tales from the Sexual Underground, and browsing through past posts, he found this one, which suited his current situation almost eerily perfectly.

## "Red Lining"

The writer sits alone on the train, thinking how the stops between North and Clybourn and Fullerton will bring him from darkness into light: a metaphor for heaven. There's a book open on his lap, something by Henry James or James Joyce, who knows? The obtuse words and their connections evoke little response when his blood flow is heading southward. Sometimes he thinks about a quote applied to Errol Flynn and how God gave him a brain and a penis and only enough blood to run them one at a time.

You get the picture. He's sitting in the last car of the northbound train, because there's always been this vague rumor that the last car is the one to board if you're gay and want to cruise. He's never seen much evidence of this, but that doesn't mean it isn't worth giving it a whirl.

And then the book below him blurs even more as the artist boards the train and sits across from him. How does he know he's an artist? Even though the evidence is circumstantial, it's pretty convincing: he carries a battered black leather portfolio; his faded jeans are spattered fetchingly with paint in various hues. The other accoutrements: shaved head, oval rimless glasses and an expression of being elsewhere also contribute to this portrait of the artist as a young man. Wouldn't it be lovely to think that maybe he has boarded this last car for the same reasons as the writer?

And then their eyes meet and all doubt is erased. Gay men, like straight ones, may have scores of lines designed to charm and seduce, but nothing beats the language of the eyes for communicating desire. Forget the smile. There is something in this liquid connection that transcends gestures as pedestrian as words and body language. The eyes have it. The artist's are pale blue, behind the glass, and his stare, held for a few seconds longer than what's appropriate for a stranger's glance, says everything the writer needs to know.

When the train reaches Belmont, the artist gives one more meaningful glance and the writer rises to follow, clutching his James Joyce in front of his loose-fitting jeans. There is a moment when the writer wonders if he is doing the right thing, but when they get off the train, his doubts vanish like an ethereal wisp of smoke. A smile confirms what he's known all along and the artist's question of having the time to stop by seals the deal.

They walk to the artist's apartment, a studio above a store on Clark Street. They're naked in an instant, clothes falling to the floor in a frenzy. Bodies mesh. Lips connect. It's an old story, and hungry as you are for it, dear reader, the writer leaves the rest to your imagination. Think sinew, skin, muscle, and bone connecting, orifices explored, juices released. As the writer says: it's an old story.

After, you, dear reader, may wonder what his name was. How the hell should the writer know? That would spoil the reality of the writer's fantasy.

Chase stopped reading and went back to ruminating as he drew closer and closer to Mike's place.

He had loved Seattle, with its majestic mountain views, its stately pines, the serene beauty of Puget Sound, but being back here in Chicago felt *right* to him, down to his very bones. It wasn't something he could put his finger on, but the sense of familiarity was a comfort.

It wasn't until he was in the northbound red line subway tunnel that Chase noticed him, sitting right across the aisle. And seeing him, he thought of the blog post he'd just read.

Something, that indescribable feeling of being watched, Chase supposed, had caused him to turn his head away from staring out the window and direct his attention back to the car's interior.

A man sat across from him, and the guy gave Chase a very pointed stare. The look wasn't rude. Chase knew exactly what it was—he was being cruised. It used to happen all the time, Chase suddenly remembered, on the L. So much so, that he and Toby had once talked about the rampant cruising that occurred on the trains, calling them "sixty-second love affairs." A whole relationship could be played out in just a short passage of time, all in the language of eyes meeting and tentative smiles. It was always a boost for the ego, but it seldom went anywhere and certainly not after he had met Toby.

Chase tossed the guy a grin to see how he would react. The guy's gaze flickered away for a second, and a flush of crimson rose to his cheeks.

But then he met Chase's eyes once more and smiled back. Chase had to admit he liked the looks of the guy. He glanced back at his own reflection in the train car glass to see what had drawn the guy. Chase had assumed, even at age thirty-six, he looked simply like a tired and nondescript older man. But the face looking back at him wasn't all that bad, not really. His close-cropped dark-brown hair looked good, recently shorn at one of the Rudy's barbershops scattered around Seattle's north side, and his green eyes were alert, vibrant even. His outfit of Old Navy hoodie and jeans made him appear younger—maybe, if he dared think it—in his twenties.

He saw, he thought, what Toby must have seen, and now what this guy across from him was seeing and appeared to be interested in.

Chase turned back, and the guy continued to stare. He was cute, about six foot two, nice build, with short light-brown hair and a three- or four-day growth of beard on his face. He looked like one of the many Irish inhabiting the city. He wore a Roosevelt University T-shirt, a Carhartt jacket, and a pair of faded dungarees hanging over a pair of beat-up New Balance running shoes.

And the thing that Chase loved most? He had a worn paperback on his lap—a copy of *Anna Karenina*. The book had always been one of Chase's favorites, since he had read it first for a Russian literature class in his aborted attempt to get a college education, lo those many years ago. He had reread it several times since then and was always blown away by the tragic story. He liked that this guy had a copy, because Chase thought it marked him as a romantic, even if he was cruising him on an L train.

They stayed in their seats, of course, but the flirtation with the eyes continued as the train rumbled forward. Chase wondered what he was doing. He hadn't flirted with another guy in God knew how long. Toby had consumed his world, and although it wasn't quite true that he never noticed other guys, it was always just a passing thing, like swiveling his head to check out a shirtless runner on Green Lake Way as he drove along the lake, or noticing movie stars like Clive Owen or Gerard Butler.

He couldn't remember the last time he had actively done the gay-male mating dance made up of surreptitious looks, shy smiles, and occasionally, if one was bold or crude enough, a subtle brush of the hand across one's crotch.

Besides, he was on his way to Mike's, Toby's old best friend. What did he think would come of this, anyway?

*Does anything have to come of it, Chase? Can't you just relax and enjoy this silly moment of eye-to-eye romance with a good-looking stranger? Can't you just appreciate this handsome man in this moment of time without wondering what it means or where it will go? How about just savoring being ogled yourself? You can still pull the looks! And from hotties like this one!* Chase grinned at his thoughts. The stranger across the way, thinking the smile was meant for him, returned it.

Before they knew it, they were pulling into the busy station at Belmont Avenue. Just east of the station lay the neighborhood known as Boys Town, with its plethora of gay bars and one notorious bathhouse. Halsted Street, the epicenter of the community, was lined with rainbow pylons, the city's way of recognizing its gay citizens. Chase was trying to remember how many more stops it was to Bryn Mawr when the stranger across from him stood, looked at him pointedly, and headed for the exit door.

The two men had already had a complete conversation using only the language of the eyes, which was eloquent and to the point. There was no doubt in Chase's mind that he was attracted to the guy, and he was sure the feeling was mutual. He was kind of sad to see him go, to see their brief affair come to a close.

But the man continued to stare, grinning, as the train slowed, pulling into the station. For one panicked moment, Chase thought he was laughing at him and he had read him all wrong, but then the guy jerked his head toward the door. Chase cocked his head, eyebrows together in confusion.

The guy lifted his hand slightly and made a barely noticeable come hither motion with his hand.

*Good Lord! He wants me to follow him off the train! This is too much. I can't do this.* Chase felt giddy, a potent brew of panic, curiosity, and lust coursing through him like an electric current. *You need to get to Mike's. You're not really thinking of doing this?* another voice inside his head chided, one that sounded suspiciously like his mother.

Feeling a bunch of butterflies release in his gut and begin fluttering around, batting their wings against his insides, Chase gathered up his duffel and backpack and headed up the aisle toward the handsome stranger.

The guy gave him a relieved smile and turned toward the doors, which were just about to open.

Chase followed him off the train, thinking there was still time to hop back on and forget this nonsense.

He thought that until the doors closed and the train left the station. He turned back to his new friend.

"I don't usually do things like this," the guy said, extending his hand. "My name's Dan."

"Ah, I bet you say that to all the guys you pick up on the L." Chase gave Dan a big smile to let him know he was teasing and shook his hand. The connection, only a handshake, was hot and freighted with desire. Neither, it seemed, wanted to let go. "I'm Chase. Just got into town from Seattle."

"First time here?" Dan let go of Chase's hand and fell into place behind the other commuters heading for the stairs that would take them down to the exit.

"No, no. I lived here for, God, like a decade. I just came back to visit an old friend."

Downstairs, as people flowed around them in the busy station, Dan swallowed and said, "Now that I've got you, I'm not sure what to do with you." His grin was the sexiest thing Chase had seen in a long time. Dan scratched the back of his neck and took a quick look around him. He leaned in closer. "I know the proper thing to do is to ask you to go over to Halsted and grab a beer or something with me."

"What's the improper thing?"

Dan laughed. "Fortunately or unfortunately, depending on your perspective, I usually go with the improper thing." He paused for a moment. "So I'll just say it. You wanna come by my place for a little bit?" His whole expression could be boiled down into one word, hope, as he waited for Chase's response.

*What will I say to Mike? How will this look to him? I can't do this!* Chase replied, "Sure. Where are you?"

"Over on Roscoe. Follow me."

And Chase did. Along the way, he took out his cell phone and called Mike, telling him there'd been a small delay. Mike wanted details, but Chase cut him off with a quick "Later" and disconnected.

\*

Dan's apartment was a tiny studio overlooking Roscoe. Because he was on the fourteenth floor, facing north, you could just see the friendly confines of Wrigley Field from his two windows.

But Chase wasn't there to take in the view, or drink the beer Dan offered, or even to talk.

As they left the elevator and Chase watched the rise and fall of Dan's full, firm ass, something animal in him took over. Conscious thought flew out the window or maybe his brain simply went on autopilot as the blood flow in his body directed itself southward, resulting in one of the firmest, almost painful, erections he could remember ever having. Boners like the one he had as he followed Dan into the studio Chase had mistakenly believed were the exclusive province of his teenage years.

Chase barely waited for the preliminaries to be over. He said nothing as Dan gestured around the little room he called home, pointing out the kitchen in one corner, the living/bedroom opposite it, his glass and chrome computer desk and atop it, a laptop, closed. He merely shook his head when Dan asked if he wanted something to drink.

When it seemed Dan had run out of words to say to this man whom, after all, he barely knew, Chase pounced on the opportunity.

And on Dan.

He pushed him up against the door and kissed him. This was no gentle pressing of the lips, no tender exploration. This was a full-throttle assault, born of lust and impatience, having had the whole L ride and walk over here to build up. Chase forced Dan's willing lips open with his tongue and reamed out his mouth, tongue moving over his teeth, his gums, stopping only to duel with Dan's own probing tongue. And while they kissed, the men frantically pressed their bodies together, as if getting close enough was an impossible goal. Chase slid his hand under Dan's shirt, delighted to find a rock-hard stomach that felt as if someone had secreted a cache of cobblestones beneath the smooth skin. Rising up, he caressed Dan's pecs, firm and smooth, the nipples erect, begging to be caressed and licked. Chase did just that, pushing up the shirt and dropping his forward like a cow lowering its head to graze. With his teeth, he teased the nipples away from the muscular flesh beneath them, tickling them with the tip of his tongue and biting down gently—and then harder. Dan cried out into the wan darkness, lit only by lights from the street, gripping Chase's head and thrusting his crotch upward to grind into Chase.

Chase finally pulled away, stepping back to regard Dan and struggling to catch his breath. The passion had served only to make his new friend more alluring, bringing a very fetching blush to his cheeks and a glimmer to his eyes. Chase wondered if the physical manifestations of desire Dan displayed were matched in his own face. He was certain they were.

"You wanna get more comfortable?" Dan asked, trying to catch his breath.

In reply, Chase began stripping off his clothes, flinging them to the floor in a rush, grinning wickedly at Dan as he did the same thing. It seemed to take about five seconds for both men to be standing naked before the other.

Chase said, "My God, under those baggy clothes you were hiding quite a prize." His gaze flickered downward. "And quite a package." Dan was a David, an Adonis formed from bronze flesh. He was smooth, nearly hairless, making it easy to see the definition of muscle that crowned his shoulders, chest, arms, stomach, and even his legs. Chase felt a low growl, almost involuntary, issue from his throat. "Work out much?"

"I try." Dan's gaze flickered shyly to the floor.

"I have to taste this." Chase was shocked for a moment at his own boldness, but the fire of his lust quickly replaced his propriety as he dropped to his knees. Dan's cock jutted out in front of him. Chase touched it, wrapping his fingers around it to revel in its girth, to feel the solidity—the hardness he had caused. He estimated the dick to be about eight inches, with a circumference that wasn't all that much less than that. Dan's shaft was topped with a big head that reminded Chase of a purple helmet.

Chase closed his eyes, opened his mouth, and sank down on Dan's dick, taking it almost all the way to the root in one nimble gulp. Dan moaned. Chase brought his head up and then down again, nestling his nose in Dan's pubes, taking in a lungful of his clean, manly essence. He bobbed up and down on the stiff member, alternating tempo and stroke, taking time to lick the shaft and gently gnaw on its tip. The head of Dan's dick twitched at the back of his throat. "Oh fuck, that's good," Dan whimpered. "I hate to say this, but I don't know how much longer I can hold out."

Chase removed his mouth from Dan's dick long enough to say, "Go for it. You're a young guy; I bet I can milk a couple loads out of you before it's all over." Chase glanced briefly down at his own cock, straining upward from between his spread and hairy thighs as if it too was about to blast off. A steady stream of precome leaked from its slit, puddling on the hardwood floor below him.

Chase returned to the job at hand, using every trick he had ever learned in his life as a gay man when it came to cock sucking: using his hand to stroke as he sucked, tightening his lips around the head before suddenly opening them to admit the cock deep into the back of his throat, and moving almost all the way off, before plunging downward, over and over again.

It was only moments before Dan was crying out into the darkened room. Chase rocked back on his heels, holding tightly to the rigid dick as it spasmed, sending out pulse after pulse of creamy come that coated his cheeks, his neck, his chest and stomach. It seemed the flow was endless. But it finally did dribble to a close, along with Dan's grunts and near screams.

Chase looked down at his hairy chest, messy with come. A drop of it dripped off one nipple to land on his thigh. He laughed.

Dan clutched the wall behind him, shuddering with the last dregs of what Chase could tell was a hugely powerful orgasm.

Chase rubbed the come around on himself and looked up at Dan. "That was great. But I'm not finished with you yet."

Chase rose and took Dan's hand to lead him to the bed. Dan's come glued their hands together, and the bed was an unmade mess, the comforter balled up at one side, the mattress ticking showing where the fitted sheet had come off at one end. Dan must be a restless sleeper...or something.

Chase hooked his leg into the crook behind Dan's knees, forcing him to fall over backward on the bed. Dan looked up at him, a grin playing about his features, eyes vibrant with desire, even in the half-light.

"Lay back," Chase grunted. Dan complied, pulling the pillow under his head and lying on his back with his knees raised. His dick was already stirring back to life. Chase thought he had seldom seen such a pretty sight.

"I wanna fuck you," Chase whispered. The words caught him by surprise, since he usually bottomed, but the heat in the room and the fact that he couldn't remember his last orgasm made the need to be inside Dan fierce.

"Lube and rubbers are in the shoebox under the bed."

Chase stooped to pull out the shoebox, glancing briefly inside as he gripped the Trojans and the Wet. Dan also had a couple of dildos in there, a can of Crisco, several cockrings, and a bottle of poppers, which Chase also grabbed. He threw them on the bed near Dan's head. "You might want those."

Dan grinned and took a deep hit in each nostril as Chase unrolled the condom over his dick and then lubed it up.

"Fuck me, Daddy," Dan whimpered and raised his legs up, reaching down with both hands to pull his ass cheeks apart to reveal its pucker. The hole was shaved and tantalizingly pink, its smoothness an invitation. Chase felt he could just about shoot at the sight of it.

Grasping one ankle in each hand and positioning himself between Dan's thighs, Chase let Dan's legs rest on his shoulders as he pressed the head of his cock against Dan's opening.

"Put some lube in my ass." Dan moved back slightly, away from Chase's throbbing cock.

"Sorry." Chase put a generous dollop of the slippery stuff on a couple fingers and swabbed Dan's hole with it. "Ready?"

"What do you think?" Dan squirmed down on the bed, so that Chase's dick was positioned perfectly for entry. Chase grabbed Dan's cock in one hand, which had again grown hard, and stroked it gently as he eased first the head of his cock in, and then, inch by inch, the shaft, not stopping the forward momentum until his pubes were resting against the silky skin of Dan's ass.

Dan's eyes fluttered closed, then opened again and locked with Chase's. "Don't go easy. Hard. Fuck me hard."

And Chase did. His hips and cock pounded Dan with wild abandon, equal parts desire and grief. It barely registered in his conscious mind how long it had been since he had connected with another human being in this way, and now that he was, well, hungry wasn't a strong enough word to describe the emotion coursing through him. He had been starving and hadn't even known it.

And now he was ravenous.

The pounding went on for twenty minutes, a half hour, maybe more, the room filled only with the sound of flesh slapping against flesh and each man's groans, cries of pleasure, and panting breath.

They both clung to each other as they simultaneously came. Chase felt like something ripped inside him, but it was not an unpleasant sensation, rather almost a wild, delirious thing, a release of more than just body, but one of spirit. From Dan's shuddering and jerking, he assumed Dan's climax was almost as powerful.

Panting, Chase lowered his sweat-slicked body on top of Dan's and kissed him. He pulled back up and stared into his eyes.

Almost immediately, an ineffable sadness engulfed him. The sex had been wonderful, truly amazing, but now that it was over the room felt empty and cold. He could smell the butyl nitrate from the poppers lingering in the air. Dan looked back at him, a lazy grin across his undeniably handsome face, yet Chase couldn't help but think the man was a stranger.

*Did I use him? No, don't think that way. If you used him, he used you. It's okay.*

Chase pulled himself up and sat on the edge of the bed, staring down at the dust-covered hardwood floor, noticing the stack of gay porn DVDs on the floor next to the TV/DVD player combo, the stack of dishes in the sink, waiting to be washed. Upstairs, he heard the sound of someone flushing a toilet.

Dan rose, draping himself around Chase, and the touch, even after all they had just done, felt foreign and strange. Dan rubbed his hands over Chase's chest, nipped his ear, and whispered, "Maybe you could stay the night? I think I'm good for at least two more times."

Chase laughed, but it felt hollow. He turned to Dan, scooting away so their bodies were separate, and said, "As irresistible as that offer is, I really have to go." He frowned and ran his hand over the top of Dan's stubbled head. "My friend up in Edgewater is probably wondering what the hell happened to me. I was supposed to just take the train from the airport to his place." He laughed. "Got waylaid, I suppose." He stared hard into Dan's eyes. "Thanks so much for having me over...for everything. You don't know how much it meant to me."

Chase didn't want to bring the moment down by explaining all the backstory, so he just left it at that.

"I'm glad. You're a hot man. How long are you staying?"

"Just the week. We're doing IML over the weekend. You going?"

"Oh yeah. I never miss it."

They both laughed, low and conspiring.

"Maybe we'll bump into each other again."

Dan kissed Chase's nose. "I'll hold you to that." They paused. There was nothing more to say, really. Chase stood.

"You can take a shower if you want."

"I think I'll just wipe off a bit and get on my way."

"Okay," Dan lay back on the bed and Chase had the sudden feeling that this scene, here in this little, dirty apartment, probably repeated itself several times over every week. Dan had already dismissed him.

Chase hurried into the tiny bathroom, where he could barely turn around, and rinsed himself off, drying with a towel he found on the floor, one that looked like it could use a good washing.

# Chapter Eight

Chase found his way back to the Belmont L station and climbed the stairs to await the arrival of the next northbound Red Line train. As he peered down the long platform, dotted here and there with other commuters, searching for the headlight in the distance, he wondered what he had just done.

*Why? Why did you let that happen?*

In his mind's eye, he tried to see Toby, yearning for even a disapproving expression on his face, but when tried to conjure up his image, all Chase could manage was a human form with a blank face. There was no judgment, for sure, but there was nothing else either—things like love, compassion, and forgiveness.

While he knew it wasn't technically cheating, Toby was, after all, no longer even alive, Chase struggled with shame and guilt.

*That was so not like you. Even when you were single and things like that did occasionally happen, it was rare. What the hell got into you?*

Chase felt his lips rise on either side in a sad smile. He knew what had gotten into him—it had been two months, maybe a little more, since he had physically connected with another man. And that other man had been Toby. For the last several years, ever since they'd made a commitment to each other, it had always been Toby.

These days, Chase had been too busy nursing his broken heart after losing him to think much about sex. When the need for it had arisen, he had dispensed with it by plopping down in front of the computer, finding some free gay Internet porn, usually on Pornhub, and efficiently and hastily whacking off onto a few squares of toilet paper appropriated for just that purpose. The whole process took less than a minute usually, and left Chase feeling empty. It was no different than having a bowel movement or eating a piece of cabbage.

Now, he realized he was giving himself crumbs when he wanted a meal.

*And so, is that what you just had—a meal? It sure didn't taste like one, nor did it provide the kind of satisfaction a meal would. I feel like, even when I do hook up, all that will ever remain for me are crumbs.*

Chase didn't think he'd ever had a meal that was so unsatisfying, despite the sex being frenzied and hot. Dan was honestly one of the most gorgeous men he had ever laid eyes on. If he hadn't just fucked the hell out of him and had only seen him on the street, Chase would have surmised the guy was out of his league. He couldn't shake, though, the same old emptiness since that horrible, awful night of Toby's birthday party. Odd how Toby had come into the world and left it on the very same day.

But as physically drained as he was, something was missing. As soon as he had climaxed, the room had gone from being sexy seedy to just being sad and desperate, the lair of a young gay man who sought these connections out restlessly and was never satisfied, Chase assumed. Why? Because he never really found the connection he sought, the one born just as much of the heart as the groin.

Chase stopped thinking as the train pulled smoothly into the station. It was now going on nine o'clock and his car was half empty, deserted fully by the rush hour commuters who kept it jammed. Chase boarded and found a seat near the front, where he could stare out the window for the five or six stops it would take him to get to the Bryn Mawr station. Earlier, he had so anticipated seeing Mike again, but now he contemplated making as minimal a greeting as possible and then begging off for bed, claiming exhaustion.

Maybe things will look brighter in the morning.

He tried to close his eyes, to relax. Even though he was weary down to his very bones, he couldn't relax. To take his mind off his guilt, he turned once again to what was fast becoming his new best friend, *Tales from the Sexual Underground*.

He scrolled through the various posts, about all sorts of things—sex toys, sex workers, porn, fidelity, polyamory, asexualism, and more—until he found this one, which he thought was fitting.

## "My Perfect Date"

He knows me, so he knows the best time is a quiet one. We stay in. Dinner, drinks, and of course, the last part, the best part.

He starts off casually, wearing a pair of faded Levis, a white T-shirt worn soft, bare feet, hair still damp from the shower. There's a CD playing, soft, maybe Oscar Peterson conjuring up Gershwin from his piano. He's got a few candles lit, but nothing scented. The air in his apartment is clean, with a trace of the soap from his shower lingering.

We sit on the couch and he makes me a drink. He already knows what I like, a dirty martini made with vodka, heavy on the dirt. We laugh about how I like things dirty, but not too much. We keep our minds out of the gutter, at least for now.

After the drinks, the music, the light fading to purple outside, we move to the dining room. Old oak pedestal table, mismatched chairs and cream pillar candles...used before. He makes a light meal because he knows that later, we won't want anything too heavy weighing on us. A simple salad, arugula, red onion, plum tomatoes, drizzled with olive oil and balsamic vinegar. There's a chicken breast, poached in broth, lemon juice and walnuts, some rice. Strawberries with sour cream and brown sugar for dessert. A glass or two of white wine, an Alsatian Riesling.

We linger over the dinner, slow; the candles burn down. The sky outside fades from purple to navy blue, a glow to the south...city lights. We move to the bedroom, undress slowly.

He knows how to touch me. Knows where to make the pressure slippery and where to make it rough. Knows when to move slowly and when to increase the tempo and when to slow it down again...he doesn't want things to end too quickly. He knows that my nipples are sensitive and toys with them just hard enough, so I will feel the ghost of his caress in the morning. And all the while: music, orchestrated to ebb and flow, a soundtrack to our passion. We start off with Bach, Mendelssohn, end up with Crystal Method and Prodigy. Romance to filth. And he tells me, the whole time, about past lovers, knowing it excites me as much as his touch. Like the music, he starts off slow and romantic, telling me about his first love, Ron, how they were playful, in love, existing only for each other...so young. He tells me about a particular New Year's Eve, in a darkened bedroom in Florida, high on pot and champagne and bringing each other the most incredible gifts. But as our passion rises, so does the depravity. He moves on to orgies, nights with strangers fueled by Ecstasy, a frantic, furtive coupling with a Northwestern student in an alley by the L tracks one night in August, fucking each other sweatily while the train crackled and roared above, its human cargo oblivious. He tells me about backroom sex, the smell of poppers, leather, cum, and spit in the air, groping, being groped, connecting with shadows. He tells me everything, moving faster and faster, until even his tales and touch blur and I offer up my seed; it covers my belly in viscous arcs.

And I roll over and look at him...in the mirror. He is me.

He is me.

He wondered if he'd landed on that particular post as a kind of warning. *Should I content myself with the amorousness of Mr. Thumb and his four sons?* At that thought, Chase found himself chuckling.

As the train neared the stop that would bring him to Mike's place, he'd started looking forward to seeing him—and that felt good. It was as though a piece of him—the one that made him experience simple joy—had gone missing and now it was back. How long it would stay was anyone's guess, but at least it was here now and that's all anyone could ask for, really.

Ages had passed since he'd spent time with Mike (other than the most recent time, but that was so marred by tragedy that it simply couldn't count). When Mike had made the trip west to Seattle, both Chase and Mike believed and looked forward to the happy reunion, but now the memory of Mike's last time with him was choked, clouded over by sadness, forever stained by the horror of sudden loss.

It was time to replace that sadness with some new, happier memories.

Chase leaned his head back against the hard plastic of the seat, drew his backpack and duffel near, and closed his eyes. This time, he did allow himself to experience a tiny sensation of contentment and relaxation.

It seemed only a second or two had passed when he heard the mechanical voice announce, "Next stop is Bryn

Mawr. In the direction of travel, doors open on the left at Bryn Mawr."

Chase gathered up his things and headed out into the brisk May night. A light drizzle had begun to fall.

Stepping off the L into Mike's Edgewater neighborhood gave Chase a rush of familiarity. The traffic-clogged street, the smell of the lake just a couple blocks over, the rumble of the L on its tracks above the street—all of these things gave Chase a kind of contentment married to a bittersweet sorrow.

This city was where he'd met his first real love, and nothing could ever change that. And Chase wouldn't want to, anyway.

*

"Well, it's about time you got here!" Mike bellowed as he opened the door wider to admit Chase. "What happened? Did you meet some hottie on the train?"

Chase let loose an embarrassing titter as he swept by Mike, not answering, surprised at how quickly his old friend had nailed the truth. But then, Mike was no stranger to such situations. He had always proclaimed he was a total pig and damn proud of it. Chase knew there'd be no judgment from Mike, yet still he was reluctant to spill the details. The hookup was still shrouded in a kind of shame.

"Can I get a hug before the interrogation starts?" Chase set down his bags on the floor and turned to Mike, arms out.

In reply, Mike gathered Chase into his arms and pulled him close. For the second time that night, Chase felt his body pressed against a wall of man muscle, a grizzled face rough against his neck. Mike squeezed him so hard it almost hurt, but Chase was grateful for the enthusiasm and the closeness that somehow, even in these few seconds, was freighted with more meaning than the hour of hot sex he had just had. He took in a lungful of Mike's essence, clean and sweet, with just a slight undercurrent of perspiration. Chase knew Mike never wore deodorant; he had often said he liked men to smell like men and would turn away anyone who, as he put it, "stank of perfume."

They stood for what seemed like a minute or more, wordless, holding each other close. There was more "said" in those few silent moments than Chase thought they could find words for. There was comfort, an acknowledgment of the other's loss, and a kind of melancholy joy at being two people who had shared a tragedy. Sometimes, Chase mused, words were such insufficient tools for how we really felt. Sometimes, just a simple human touch could communicate more than a whole book.

Finally Chase broke away, moving into the condo. He drank in the elegant interior. Mike may have been a brute, a butch guy, a he-man, but he sure knew his decorating. The condo was mostly one big living area, with gleaming hardwood floors and a slate-tiled, floor-to-ceiling fireplace dominating the space. Mike had painted the walls a creamy pale yellow, almost white, that made the abstract expressionist prints on the wall and the cleanly designed minimalist furniture stand out. The white trim and crown molding lent an air of elegance to the space.

"Wow. Looks like you're ready for *Architectural Digest* to come in and start shooting." Chase eyed the narrow floor to ceiling windows, four of them along the east wall. Darkness pressed in against the glass, but Chase knew in the morning there would be a glorious view of Lake Michigan.

Mike followed him into the room, flipped a switch on the wall to set off the flames in the gas fireplace. "Speaking of shooting, was I right? About your train ride?" Mike grinned, retreating into the open kitchen, waiting for his answer across the top of a black granite counter.

Chase felt heat rise to his face. "C'mon, Mike. You wouldn't want me to kiss and tell, would you? I'm too much a gentleman for that."

"You wanna beer?" Without waiting for an answer, Mike threw open the doors on his stainless steel refrigerator, removing two chilled bottles of Stella Artois.

"My favorite. You remembered." Chase eyed the beer. The cold green glass looked inviting.

Mike used an opener to pop the tops and winked. "Yeah, that's right. Your favorite. Let's go with that." He crossed over to Chase and handed him his beer. They clinked bottles and took a swig.

"So?"

Chase stared down at the cherry hardwood floor, noticed how the flames from the fireplace threw a flickering light upon its surface. "So, yeah. I got laid." All of a sudden, Chase felt a ball form in his throat and hot tears spring to the corners of his eyes. He had to force himself to breathe, because it seemed all the air was rushing out of him, like a pricked balloon. *What's wrong with me?* He wiped the tears quickly away with the back of one hand. "You think that's okay?"

"Okay? I think it's fabulous. Wait. Don't tell me..." Mike took in Chase's expression, and Chase knew he could see the fresh tears. "Was it your first time since..." Mike's voice trailed off, and Chase realized they both knew what he was talking about. Mike hugged him, patting his back. "It's okay, hon. It's normal. Both the hookup and how you're feeling right now."

Chase took another swig of beer. A big one. Its icy cold was the perfect antidote for the weird guilt and grief that had risen up, unbidden and of its own accord, out of nowhere. "Yeah. I've been a bit of an old maid. Cobwebs encasing my balls..."

Both men broke into laughter.

Mike put his arm around Chase and led him to the couch. "Well, this weekend is going to change everything. Let's just sit and get comfortable, and you can tell Daddy all about it."

*

Later, as Chase tossed and turned under the covers, he vacillated between: *Should I be here? Should I be back in Seattle? Where's home?*

He didn't think he'd sleep, but before he knew what was happening, his eyelids fluttered shut and his mouth opened to emit a buzz-saw-like snoring.

*He's in one of those tunnels that cross underneath Lake Shore Drive. Not sure what time of day it is, but the sky has a gray and lavender illumination.*

*The tunnel itself is dark and foreboding.*

*But Chase feels he must cross through it to get to the other side. Even though he could go around, straight through is easier.*

*Besides, there's a figure ahead and he looks okay. Safe.*

*Chase quickens his pace as the figure ahead slows his own stride.*

*They're nearing the end of the tunnel now, and the sky is like a dull grayish rectangle, a blank movie screen.*

*The figure turns.*

*He has no face.*

*It's Toby.*

*Chase raises a hand toward him.*

*But Toby turns again and walks away, faster now. Into the gloom.*

*He vanishes.*

*All of the sudden, the sound rushes in—the roar of traffic above, busily heading north and south. He can even hear the sound of the surf as it hurls itself against the boulders at the shoreline.*

*Where's Toby?*

*Where is everyone?*

*The lakefront is deserted as he emerges from the tunnel, and the world goes silent again.*

Chase woke with a start, tangled in damp sheets. He cries out one word, "Toby!" It's a strangled yell. His gaze moves to the closed door, where a strip of light runs along its bottom. Soft patter of bare feet. A shadow breaks up the light.

Mike stood outside for a moment, listening. And then he moved on.

# Chapter Nine

## "The Truth—and the Myths—About Being a Slut"

It's not easy being a slut. Maligned, judged, and often misperceived, we sluts are often thought of as having no values, when the opposite is true: most sluts are filled with the milk of human kindness (or some fluid like that)—that's why we end up being called sluts. So I've come up with this list of truths and falsehoods about being a slut in an effort to educate the public on this often misunderstood segment of our populace.

**A slut will sleep with *anybody*.** False! Sluts often have very high standards. Just because we've been the pleasure connection to thirty gentlemen in one weekend doesn't mean that we weren't choosy. Just lucky...

**A slut thinks about sex all the time.** True. If you're a good, practicing slut, most other concerns of life take a backseat (as you often do!) to when, where, and with whom you'll have your next orgasm.

**A slut has low self-esteem**. Bullshit. Whoever started this line of malarkey was just jealous. Sluts simply realize what a gift their sexual organs are and are unselfish enough not to hold those gifts back from worthy admirers.

**A slut is like a Petri dish, growing all sorts of nasty bacteria and viruses on their person**. Well, this is both true and false. An inescapable reality of sluthood is that it's like playing Russian Roulette. Sooner or later, you're going to come down with a bug or two. But good sluts realize this and make it a point to know what preventative measures they can take and visit their doctors regularly.

**A slut preys on the young.** Yeah, right. Does that make Bill Clinton a slut? Wait, don't answer that. A true slut knows that tasty sexual partners come in all shapes, sizes…and ages. Youth has its charms, but with age comes experience, wisdom, and hopefully, control…

**A slut just can't get enough**. True. And what's wrong with that? Sex feels good. It's making someone else feel good, so where's the problem? If you're slut, you know that enough is never enough, unless it's right after. Then a cigarette or a bowl of Ben and Jerry (the ice cream!) sounds a whole lot better than having a big howitzer stuffed up some juicy orifice. Or does it?

**Sluts smell bad**. False. A slut, more than anyone else, knows that a clean pussy (or butthole, or cock and balls) is a sexy pussy.

**Sluts are open-minded**. True. A real slut knows there's no end to sexual pleasure and what can bring it on, thus she or he doesn't limit herself or himself to discovering the joy that a particular mammal, battery-operated device, latex lovely, fruit/veg, etc. can bring.

**Sluts make bad husbands or wives**. False. A true self-proclaimed slut has learned a thing or two about honesty, being true to yourself, and being communicative about needs. All those things add up to knowing how to make a relationship work.

**Sluts are the answer to world peace**. True. So true. Who do you think coined the phrase: make love, not war?

So, sluts unite...again and again and again. And let me know where you're uniting (and if you have a sling). Slut Pride...it's time has come.

*

Chase felt a sense of déjà vu as he and Mike headed downtown to the Hyatt Regency the next morning. That first time he had gone to the event came back to him in vivid Technicolor imagery.

That Saturday had been much like this one: cool, sunny, with the train half full of "regular folks," students, people going shopping on Michigan Avenue, the homeless staking out a place to be for a few hours, and the leather crowd sprinkled throughout the car. They wouldn't have looked out of place at a leather bar on Halsted or North Clark, but here, on this sunny day of a holiday weekend, they stuck out.

It was nice, though, that no one seemed to care.

Chase realized how much he missed this big city. The wonderful thing about big cities were one, people often just didn't give a fuck about others, which could work in your favor or against it. And two, you could be invisible in a metropolis and that also worked both ways, but it certainly had the potential to keep life interesting.

He had many of the same feelings he had experienced way back when attending IML for the first time. He was anxious with anticipation, a little fear, and a vague sense of something completely unexpected heading his way. There was a bit of dread, but that was tempered with a lot more of "kid on Christmas morning." What would be wrapped up and under the tree for Chase?

It was as though the train was traveling not only in space, but in time, taking him into a future that had the possibility of changing him. Was change a good thing?

Chase turned to Mike, who was seated along the aisle. "So, what's your agenda for the day look like?" He knew the probability was very high that he and Mike might at some point get separated. Law of the jungle—if one of you found a hot guy, all bets were off.

"Thought we'd hit the hotel bar first."

Chase cut him off. "The bar?" He looked down at his watch. "Honey, it's only eleven o'clock!"

Mike rolled his eyes. "Not so much for a drink, although you do what you want, I'm having a big Bloody as soon as I sit down, but more to check out the scene and the men." Mike winked. "They congregate there, between fucking bouts, after all-nighters and before and after power shopping the leather mart."

"Well, you're the tour guide." Chase peered out the windows at the backs of apartment buildings flashing by as the train headed south.

Mike's mention of the Leather Mart brought back memories of the big bazaar of leather gear and fetish toys. He hadn't been to events like the Folsom Street Fair in San Francisco, but wondered if there was anything in the world that matched an IML Leather Mart for sheer kinkiness per square foot. It wasn't so much all the different booths that had so many things on display, some verging toward the hardcore and extreme, things like stainless steel sounds, which were tubes in graduated sizes for insertion into the urethra, water sports, and bondage DVDs, things like purple wands to send an electric shock through the person it was being used on, but all the people there. People of like minds. Chase thought of them all as libertines, sexual adventurers. And they were on display as much as the wares of the vendors. His other head rose a little, both from the gentle rocking motion of the train and from Chase flashing on the hordes of hot leather men who would be milling around the hotel bar and the leather mart, some dressed scandalously in as little as a rubber jock strap.

Mike poked a finger into Chase's side. "What are you thinking about?" He grinned, almost leering, as though he could read Chase's mind.

"Not much."

"Listen, I wanted to tell you, since you asked about *my agenda* that you're free to roam around on your own; don't feel like you have to stick by my side the entire time."

"Oh, I know. That's one of the things I was pondering. But...are you sure you're not just saying that for your own benefit, Mike?" Chase raised his eyebrows. "You don't need to. You're a free agent."

"Well, yeah, I suppose. But sincerely, it's for both of us. You might see a party you want to go to, different groups are having them throughout the day and night and I'm sure," Mike paused to look Chase up and down, "you'd be welcome at each and every one of them. And no, they don't necessarily have to be orgies." Mike winked. "Although I'd be lying if I said those weren't my favorite kind of parties."

Chase took stock of himself, not quite believing he was dressed as he was, out in public on a Saturday morning, but Mike had insisted. That morning, Mike had rummaged through the clothes Chase had brought, rejecting almost everything as too "Mary Poppins" for the leather high holidays.

Mike finally settled on a pair of old, ripped up Levi's Chase had brought and paired them with Mike's own skintight pewter Latex vest that zipped up in the front, studded leather armbands for each arm, and a leather baseball cap. "You can just turn the bill backwards if you find a cock you want to suck," Mike had joked. Chase knew there was some seriousness mixed in with the jest. Fortunately, he had brought along a pair of worn combat boots that were as comfortable as a pair of sneakers.

"Anyway," Mike continued. "Just so you know, if we do get separated, you can always text or call, so we can be in touch. It's the beauty of our 21st century tracking devices. And if the other doesn't answer, we should each wait a respectful amount of time before calling back. But even if we go our separate ways, I do want us to have dinner together tonight. I remembered how much you liked North Pond over in Lincoln Park, so I made us a reservation for seven. That way, we can check out the mart, have a little fun, however we define it, then come home, catch a nap, shower, change, go to dinner, and then come back and relax before we head out to the bars tonight."

Chase snorted. "You talk like we're still in our twenties! Hey, with Toby and me the past several years, we were often in bed by eleven on Saturday nights, and weeks, sometimes months, would pass without us setting foot in a gay bar."

Mike's face grew serious. "Toby isn't here anymore. And, not to be insensitive, but you're single now. Remember that this weekend." The words might have seemed harsh if Chase hadn't witnessed the caring in his friend's eyes, or the quick, gentle way Mike touched Chase's cheek. Mike had only good intentions.

*

Chase was exhausted. The day had been a blur, a whirlwind defined by leather, latex, and rubber. Much as that first time he attended this event, Chase was once again surprised by all the attention he got. Men tried to catch his eye, turning their heads to peer at him as he walked by, or they sidled up to him, whispering things like "Woof" and "You're hot" in his ear.

It was all good for his ego, until he realized these guys were most likely saying the same things and giving the same looks to half the crowd. Still, the day had been more fun than he had thought it would be. It was charged with an almost electric sense of sexual tension, but there was also this pervasive atmosphere of fun, of liberation. Inside the walls of this very conventional hotel, people were free to behave and look exactly the way they wanted without fear of reproach, or worse. Chase thought it was kind of a contained Disneyland for adults.

And now, as Chase sat here in the Hyatt's bar, nursing a Stella Artois, he looked back on the day with satisfaction, glad he'd taken the time off from work and come back home to Chicago. He felt both guilty and relieved as he realized, for the first time in a long time, that he had not thought of Toby, that he had not pined for his presence by his side. It was sad, because it meant maybe he was letting go, just a little bit. But it was also a small cause for joy, because it also meant, just maybe, that he was getting back on the road to life once more.

Chase took a sip of his beer and looked around at all the men, clustered in pairs or groups, laughing and talking. Although he sat alone at the bar, he felt like he was one of them. There were even a few scattered here and there among the crowd with whom he had flirted, as he and Mike made several circuits through the leather mart.

He was no longer, as he'd often felt these past few months, an outsider, a stranger looking through the closed windows of life, never noticed.

Mike had wandered off yet again, this time with a burly, shaved-head guy with so many tattoos it was almost hard to tell what color his skin was. The man actually had Chinese symbols tattooed across his forehead. He also sported multiple piercings. His oversized, beefy frame was clad only in boots and a skin-tight black latex wrestling singlet with a jolt of yellow around the zipper.

Mike thought he was just about the hottest thing he had ever seen. "Gotta get me some of that," he said out of the corner of his mouth before heading off in the guy's direction. Chase watched, amused, as Mike started talking to the guy and the obvious infatuation that fired almost immediately between the pair. And why not? Mike was just as hot in his own way—much more so, to Chase's eye—than the extreme tattoo guy.

Mike had put on a pair of leather chaps, worn jockstrap, and a studded leather harness over his furry, defined chest. He looked like he drank testosterone for breakfast. Within about five minutes, Mike and tattoo man were in a clinch, then a lip lock, and then finally heading off together, presumably to the guy's room.

Which is how Chase found himself here at the bar— on his own. It wasn't so bad. The cross-country trip and the day on his feet, full of ogling and leering, had caught up with him. It felt good just to sit here and have a minute to catch his breath. He felt no pressure to meet anyone, to make any kind of impression. He could relax and lean into simply watching and enjoying the interplay of these beautiful men. And they were *all* beautiful—regardless of age, size, shape, or color.

And besides, as hot as all the men surrounding him were and as exciting as all the possibilities they offered, his balls had been drained quite adequately the night before. His motor was revving, as it were; he just wasn't ready to shift into drive.

And that was okay.

This stool at the bar was the only place he wanted to be. He could eavesdrop, stare out the large windows at the clouds drifting by, and feel a little tingle as yet another hot man passed.

"So what's your story?"

Chase turned at the sound of the deep voice, expecting from the bass tenor to see a large man, but instead found the cutest small-statured Latino guy standing next to him and holding a beer. He had to have been no more than five five, but his frame was packed with lean muscle showed off to a good advantage by an atypical ensemble: a simple white T-shirt and a pair of Levi's, and, God forbid, a pair of Nikes. His hair was black and on the longish side for this crowd, hanging down nearly to his shoulders in silken waves. His face was chiseled, highlighted by some of the darkest brown eyes Chase had ever seen. Dark stubble framed his handsome face. Chase was mesmerized.

"My story? What?"

"Everyone has a story, right? You look like the only person in this room who's actually doing any thinking. I thought maybe I could get in on the details of what's causing that very attractive brow to furrow." The guy laughed. "The rest of us are too busy cruising, seeing who we can get in bed next. It's the leather high holidays." He snorted and chuckled as though that last line was occurring to him first.

"Ah, is that your game, then?" Chase asked. The guy was adorable, but he didn't know if he was as eager as Mike to trot off to a hotel room with a stranger.

Just then the stool next to Chase cleared and the guy climbed up on it and signaled the bartender for another beer. He pointed to Chase's half empty bottle with raised eyebrows and Chase placed a hand over the top of his bottle, saying, "I'm good."

Once the guy had his next beer in hand, he said, "I don't have a game. I do have a story, though. I just came over to see if I could get in on what you were thinking about—see what makes such a thoughtful-looking dude tick." He shrugged. "Simple." He took a swig. "So you still haven't told me."

"Ah, I don't know how interesting my story is, really." *That's a lie and you know it. Why, just the past couple months of your life are enough of a story, a tragicomedy if you will, that would hold this guy's interest.* "I don't really know how much detail you want, since we don't, at this point, even know each other's names."

"I'm Wade." Chase's new friend stuck out his hand and Chase shook it. "I know, I know. You were expecting Carlos or Juan? Maybe Jose? My parents were rebels."

"I wasn't expecting anything. It's nice to meet you, Wade. I'm Chase."

"First time at the big event?"

"Well, it's the first time in a long time. I used to come, then I got involved with someone, and we moved away— long story. I just came back to visit a friend, and he loves this stuff. So here we are. He's probably up in a room somewhere, fisting a guy or engaging in some other wholesome, all-American pastime. And I'm just chilling here until he's done."

"Didn't want to get in on the action?" Wade cocked his head.

Chase shrugged. "I don't know. A beer sounded better than a dick right now."

Wade leaned close. "Sh, don't let anyone hear you say that. Around these parts, that's blasphemy, or treason, or something. They'll run you out of town on a rail."

They both laughed.

Wade asked, "So where is it you're visiting from?"

"Seattle."

He nodded. "I always wanted to go there. From what I've seen, it looks beautiful. Don't know if I could handle all the rain, though."

"Ah, it's not so bad. Most of the time, it's a little drizzle and some gray skies. You can do whatever you want outside. It never gets too cold in the winter and rarely snows. And the summers! Man, there's nothing as perfectly gorgeous as a summer in Seattle."

For the next hour or more, the two men chatted, laughed, cajoled, and began to share in the other's *story*. Wade's warm brown eyes caused Chase to open up, and he surprised himself by telling him everything that had happened over the past couple of months. He was able to do it without even shedding a tear, which Chase chalked up as a victory.

It wasn't long before Chase noticed the sky outside beginning to deepen in hue, its color changing from pale blues to deeper navy, purple, and orange. He had gotten to know a lot about Wade. He was a waiter for one of the top-rated restaurants in the country, up near the Steppenwolf Theater; he had aspirations to be a model but feared he was too short; he had a passion for Japanese anime; and sexually, he was all bottom. "One hundred percent," he said with a wink and a grin. "Just can't get enough of that wonderful stuff." He raised a bushy eyebrow at Chase.

Chase had responded in kind, telling Wade all about his work at the animal hospital in Seattle, and how he hoped to get back to school so he could at least be a vet tech, or even better, a vet. With a steady expression and no drama, he had even managed to let Wade know all about Toby, and what had happened on his fortieth birthday.

"Man, that's rough. I can't imagine. So sudden! So young! I feel for you, man." Wade had sympathized, placing a brotherly hand on Chase's shoulder and squeezing. Chase appreciated the gesture, but had quickly changed the subject. He didn't want to get all maudlin, not now.

Just as he was wondering if Mike would ever return, or if he had lost him for the night, he saw him across the room, wading through the crowd which had grown larger as it got closer to the bar's happy hour.

Chase smiled at Wade. "Hey, man, it's been great talking to you, but I see my buddy headed this way. We're probably going to head back to his place now to get ready to go out for dinner. He's set us up for North Pond in Lincoln Park."

"Yum. Amazing place."

Chase slid off the stool as Mike drew near. He noticed, out of the corner of his eye, that Wade was scribbling something down on the back of a receipt he extracted from his wallet. His number, maybe?

"You about ready to go?" Mike had finally reached him. He leaned in close and whispered, "I can make myself scarce if you want."

"No, that's okay. I'm kind of looking forward to getting back and maybe taking a little snooze. I am definitely up for going to North Pond. I checked out the menu online and it still looks amazing." Even before he had left Chicago, the restaurant, in a beautifully restored warming shelter in Lincoln Park, had been one of Chase's favorite places.

Toby had taken him there for the first time shortly after they had started dating. And with just that thought, Chase felt a stab of pain right in his heart. He closed his eyes for a moment. *Breathe.*

He turned back to Wade. "Hey, maybe I'll see you again? We're going to be back down here tomorrow. Right, Mike?" He swiveled his stool toward Mike.

Mike smiled at Wade. "Right." He extended his hand. "I'm Mike Rogers."

"Wade Timmons. How you doin'?" They shook hands, eyeing each other up. Then Wade turned his attention back to Chase, holding out the piece of paper. "I'm having a little party at my place tonight in Ravenswood. You know, in honor of IML. I'd love it if you'd drop by. It should go pretty late, so no worries about what time you might get there." He eyed Mike once more. "You can come too, Mike."

Chase took the scrap of paper. "Thanks. That's sweet of you. I'll try. Okay?"

"Do better than that." Wade winked at him and strode away. "Show up. I promise you won't be disappointed. And who knows? Maybe you'll have another chapter to add to your story."

They said their goodbyes and started out of the bar, heading toward the elevators that would take them to the parking garage. Mike was grinning at him. "So are you gonna go?"

"Oh, I don't know. I mean, we talked, but I barely know him. I certainly wouldn't know anyone else there." It occurred to Chase that the party might not be the kind where folks mingle with their clothes on, enjoying libations and chips and dip.

"Well, his party would be a chance to get to know him better, right? And maybe meet some new people?" Mike pushed the down button outside the elevators. "You could get to know him *a lot* better, if you know what I mean."

Chase scratched his head, wondering how Mike had gotten so quickly inside his mind. "Oh, you don't think he's having some kind of sex party, do you?"

Mike smirked, shaking his head, presumably at Chase's naiveté. "Oh, you sweet boy." They stepped into the elevator and waited for the doors to close. "That's usually the kind of party you get invited to at IML. I'm just sayin'." He laughed.

"Well, I doubt it. He didn't seem like the sort."

"And what is the sort? Pigs like me?" Mike waited for a beat. "Don't answer that!"

They rode down to the parking garage in silence. A sex party? Chase didn't know if he was up for *that*.

# Chapter Ten

North Pond had been amazing. Chase had forgotten just how inspired, and delicious, the seasonal, local-ingredient food was. He and Mike had a feast for all of their senses as they dined on beet and trout salad, prawns with cauliflower mousse, goat cheese and leek strudel, and turbot with black truffle potatoes.

It had been nice to step away from the world of IML for a few hours. And it had been hot to see Mike actually *out* of his leather fetish wear and dressed in pale ecru slacks and a simple black cashmere V-neck sweater. Chase wasn't sure which way the man looked hotter.

Chase had been surprised over dinner when Mike brought up his experience with the "tattooed and pierced" guy. He had been expecting Mike to revel in some passionate, hot encounter, and there was some of that, but Mike said, "It was hot, I guess. But maybe I'm just getting old and jaded, but after it was over, it just seemed—I don't know—kind of empty." Mike took a sip of his wine. "This might sound weird, but I felt a little...sad. I don't know that I've ever felt that way before." Chase was taken aback. He had felt exactly the same about the guy he had met on the L.

"What's *that* all about?" Chase toyed with his napkin, drank some of his own wine. He knew the answer to the question, but asked because he wanted to hear how Mike would respond.

"I don't know. I'd just shared a bunch of bodily fluids with this guy, had an incredible orgasm that left me literally trembling, and yet, and yet... When it was all over, I just kind of felt like: Who are you? Is that stupid?"

"Not at all."

*

Mike's experience with the tattooed-and-pierced guy didn't seem to deter him once they got back to the apartment. Mike had quickly gotten rid of the GQ look he had sported for North Pond, and changed back into full leather gear: leather jeans, a policeman uniform shirt, tall black boots, and a leather military cap.

It was around eleven thirty when he emerged from his bedroom, looking like he was ready for a Colt photo shoot. He cocked his head at Chase, who still sat on the couch wearing what he had worn to dinner: a pair of jeans and a striped button-down shirt. He was flipping through the channels on Mike's plasma screen TV. "What's up? Aren't you going to get ready to go out? I thought we'd hit Cell Block first, see what happens from there."

Chase smiled, trying to soften the blow of what he was about to say. "You know what? I'm tired. I think I'll just stay in, if you don't mind."

"What? Are you sure? I bet once we got out, with the bars hoppin' with hot men, you'd get a second wind."

Chase shook his head. "Nah. I really think I'd be happier here. Turner Classic Movies is showing *Imitation of Life*. You don't mind, do you?"

"Listen, there will be plenty of old friends out tonight, and I suspect, some new ones too." He wiggled his eyebrows. "So I'm cool with it. If you're tired, you're tired." He walked back to his room and came back with a set of keys and handed them to Chase. "Just in case you change your mind. Public transportation is right outside the door, and you know your way around the city. Don't feel you have to stay in, or even join up with me, for that matter, although it would be nice if you did. I have my cell." Mike brushed his lips across Chase's, his tongue tickling Chase's lips but not going so far as to enter his mouth. Chase was a bit stunned. "Later."

"Have fun."

Chase listened as Mike softly closed the door behind himself. Chase turned the TV off. What had that kiss been all about? He felt if he had responded, Mike might have continued, the kiss growing more passionate. Who knew where it might have led? Chase got up from the couch and began moving around the apartment, suddenly feeling weird and a bit restless.

He and Mike were just friends, right? He had been Toby's best friend. He wouldn't be putting the moves on Chase, would he?

Chase laughed, but there wasn't much humor in it. *Mike was probably just horned up because of the weekend, you idiot. It most likely wasn't even personal. He probably would have kissed his sister like that.* Chase paused for a moment in his thoughts. *Yuck!*

Chase paused at the door to Mike's bedroom. A streetlight outside threw a slatted pattern of light and darkness across Mike's king-size bed. Its surface was covered with cast-off leather gear Mike must have tried on before settling on his cop shirt and leather jeans ensemble.

Then he spied the framed photograph on Mike's dresser. Even in the half-light, he recognized the shot, and it inspired a sort of breathless euphoria and, at the same time, sadness. He moved into the room, switched on the lamp on the nightstand, and picked up the photo.

It was of Chase and Toby. He remembered exactly when Mike had taken it. They were getting ready to leave Chicago for Seattle and had been spending their last day in the Windy City with their best friend. Mike had suggested they walk down to the lakefront, since it was a glorious autumn day. The sun shone out of a cloudless blue sky, the kind of blue one only sees in autumn, an almost surreal electric color, so deep it almost looked painted. Although the rays of the sun were hot, they contrasted with the breeze blowing off the lake, which was delightfully crisp and cool. The leaves were at their peak in terms of color, and back from the beach, oaks and maples practically shimmered in the sunlight, throwing off brilliant reds, oranges, and yellows.

That day, much like this photograph, was frozen in time, in memory. It was a time of transition, leaving a comfortable old life behind and heading out for the new and unknown. It was bittersweet. Chase loved the life he had in Chicago and, for him, more than any place else, the metropolis was *home*, a concept that had always been vital to him.

Yet the promise of new beginnings was exciting, and the fact that he was jumping into the abyss of something unknown clinging to the hand of the man he loved, erased all of his fears, if not all of his longing to stay put.

They had walked Hollywood Beach. It had a more proper name, Kathy Osterman Beach, but they had always just called it Hollywood. The waves were high that day, and the Windy City lived up to its name. Gusts nearly took their breath away and the water was whitecapped, the roar of the surf loud enough to make them shout to be heard.

And Mike had pulled from his pocket his trusty little Canon point-and-shoot digital.

"Come on, you guys. I need a good picture to remember you by, and the light right now is just perfect. Stand over there and try not to look too happy." Mike pointed to a spot where the waves and the breakwater at the southern edge of the beach would make the perfect backdrop.

Toby had slid his arm around Chase and they had angled their heads toward one another, smiling and squinting just a bit from the sun.

Chase moved a finger across the glass surface covering the photograph, remembering. Even though it was only a few years ago, they looked so much younger then. Their faces were red, wind-burned, and their hair was blown back from their faces.

The day had held so much promise, shadowed with melancholy at their early morning departure on Alaska Airlines. Chase set the photo back down.

He didn't think either of them could have imagined that one of them would be dead within a few years of that photo being taken.

He switched out the light and hurried from the room.

In the guest room, he lifted his wallet and pulled out the receipt upon which Wade had written his address and cell.

*Are you sure you want to do this? Mike was probably right; this was going to be a sex party, an all-night, all-male orgy.*

*Yet maybe Mike was wrong, and this was just a regular old party with a keg of beer and chips and dip on the table, people mingling, and talking loud over dance music.*

*Sure, right.* Chase knew he had to at least be prepared for the fact that he might be headed out to a sex party and to think about what he'd do when he got there, when he was asked to get naked with the rest of the guests.

*Really? Are you sure you want to do this?* He thought of the photo in the other room. Guilt stabbed at him, but so did another emotion, curiosity and a desire to do something that had to do with *life* and not death.

Maybe this party was the antidote, a vote for life, vibrant, sexual life. Human connection.

Perhaps it would be just what he needed.

In spite of jitters and butterflies dancing around in his gut like they were hopped up on stimulants, Chase squatted down before his duffel bag and rooted through his clothes, trying to decide what to wear.

# Chapter Eleven

## "So You Wanna Host an Orgy?"

Recently, a very nice young man wrote to me and asked if I could offer any tips on hosting an orgy. This young man was a subscriber to *Martha Stewart Living* and an avid reader of *Miss Manners* and stated that he would "simply be red-faced with shame" should he commit any group sex *faux pas*. So, for him, and others like him, I present the following common sense advice:

**Consider renting a hotel room**. The benefits of this are obvious: you don't have to worry about strangers coming into your home and taking things that you are not offering. Provided your guests aren't *too* destructive and you use some common sense with regards to just how many bodies a hotel room will comfortably hold, you can "get off" with a lot less hassle.

**Devise a plan for invitations**. This is always tricky. Do you invite friends? Strangers? Past lovers? Cousins? Funny uncles? Of course, there is some risk in opening up your party to strangers, but with orgies, this is often the case. It allows for the element of surprise. One hopes, though, that the surprises are always of the pleasant variety. There are several avenues for getting your message across, including sending out engraved invitations, utilizing Internet message boards, referring interested parties to an e-mail address for further details, handing out small, tastefully printed cards or notes at the bar of your choice on the night of the party (you can be selective this way, but don't be surprised if a few invitations happen to go astray and the troll patrol shows up at your door at 4 a.m.), utilizing the various phone sex lines that allow one to leave a message (risky because you'd need to leave your phone number so that prospective guests could all for details), or writing the details on a men's room wall (the wild card that could transport you to new heights of heaven and/or hell). Of course: the safest route to travel would be inviting people you know. Not as exciting, but a good way to avoid some nasty surprises.

**Establish ground rules**. This is your party and you can (fill in the blank) if you want to. Decide before you invite even that first person whether or not this will be a safe sex party, what kind of condoms or condiments you will, or won't, provide, what drugs, if any, are permissible and the level of attitude you'll permit with your guests. Foreknowledge with foreplay will result in the most successful parties. Once things are in motion, it's often too late to try and establish ground rules.

**Will you charge**? Sometimes, asking for a small fee to help cover your costs is permissible, provided that you're not tacky enough to be attempting to make a profit. Certainly, it's not unreasonable to ask for a small cover charge if you're providing lube, condoms, beer, Cheetos or Charmin.

**And last, but certainly not least, devise an exit plan**. As exciting as the prospect of an orgy might sound, there will come a time when you wish everyone would just get the hell out. Make sure your guests know up front when that time is and stick to it. It's always courteous to give a fifteen or so minute warning so that guests will have an opportunity to finish the business at hand or make arrangements to continue their socializing elsewhere.

Enjoy! And don't forget to invite me.

In the end, Chase decided to wear something that would be easy to get out of if Wade was, indeed, throwing *that* kind of party. And...if he decided to take the plunge and take part in such a party. That was still up in the air and Chase supposed it could go either way—he could return home, unready and relieved. Or, he could wind up with his ass up on the air, rather than his decision.

He looked down at himself: at the jeans and Old Navy Sweatshirt, the Asics running shoes. All could be removed in a minute or two. He decided against hitting up Mike for fetish wear. With Chase, it had always been what you see is what you get.

He *had* gone commando, leaving his boxer briefs on the foldout bed in Mike's office.

He was once again aboard the L train. He had considered grabbing a cab; they were easy to get on Sheridan Road, a block from Mike's condo, but he reminded himself that he didn't make the kind of money to go gallivanting around in a taxi—or even an Uber, not when the L was such a bargain. Honestly, door to door via the L train was not only cheaper, but faster and more direct than subjecting himself to Chicago traffic. A ride to Wade's Ravenswood neighborhood would cost him at least twenty bucks, as opposed to a few dollars for the train. So what if he had to change from the red line to the brown at Belmont, then ride back north to Western Avenue? The time alone, he supposed, would give him to think it through.

And he was in a constant state of reconsidering. One minute, he thought going to a sex party, if that was, indeed, where he was headed, was a betrayal to Toby's memory. It would be pain, rather than pleasure he'd feel in such a setting.

And then he'd bounce back and decide he needed to *live,* and embracing a few hot men on a spring night might be just the kind of distraction he needed, a balm to his grief.

As the train pulled into Western, Chase continued to try to make up his mind, over and over again, first thinking he should just head back, watch some TV, go to bed at a decent hour, and then curious about what lay at the end of his destination. He had never attended a real live sex party, and now that he was single, what reason did he have for avoiding the experience? Hell, he might come home worn out, but having had a very good time.

He was at his stop. He stepped off the train and stood frozen on the platform, watching as it pulled away. Sure, he could hop on the next southbound train, but he felt that by departing the train, he'd come to some sort of decision.

He was going ahead with this. He turned toward the exit.

He joined the other commuters on the down escalator and headed out onto busy Western Avenue. The street's four lanes were clogged with Saturday night traffic. People rushed along the sidewalks in groups and singly, heading out to catch a movie, grab a cappuccino at Starbucks, shop or have dinner in nearby Lincoln Square. The noise was constant and if Chase let go, it morphed into a single drone.

Chase couldn't help but wonder what they would think if they knew where he was headed. *Why would anyone care where you're going? You putting yourself in everyone's thoughts and judgements is beyond egotistical, for god's sake!*

He turned right at Wilson and began searching for Wade's address, among the two-flats, three-flats, and courtyard apartment complexes. Two blocks east and he found it, a redbrick three-flat with large front balconies with cream trim. It was a nice building, well maintained, that read *condo* and not the more transient, *apartment.*

He stared up at the third floor, where he knew Wade's place was located, and realized Mike was probably right. The glass of each window revealed tightly closed blinds. A dim light flickered out from behind the shades. Candles, maybe? Chase flashed on a scene of debauchery, something out of Fellini, perhaps, or imagined by the Marquis de Sade himself.

*Do you really want to do this? You can still go back, grab the train or even catch that bus that's coming toward you down Wilson. Because once you ring that buzzer and trudge up those stairs, it will be much harder to reverse the course of the evening.*

*Yeah, yeah, yeah. Shut the fuck up*, Chase told his inner voice and marched up the stairs to the front porch. There was a little vestibule that Chase ducked inside, scanning the three buzzers for the name, Timmons. His finger hesitated only briefly above the buzzer before he pressed it, with a feeling of "in for a penny, in for a pound."

After hoping no one would answer, Chase shifted his hope rapidly to praying Wade would even remember him, and his name, as he waited to be asked who was calling. But no voice came through the intercom. There was only a metallic buzz and a click to announce that the door to the inner stairs had been unlocked.

*Hmmm...I wonder if this means it doesn't matter who's arrived. Just the more, the merrier. Oh Lord, what have you gotten yourself into? Anyone could just come in from off the street. Wasn't this dangerous?*

Despite his misgivings, Chase trudged up the stairs, telling himself that he was being adventurous, open-minded, a free spirit, or as Mike would put it, a "shameless pig."

He was none of those things. Never had been? But never would? That remained to be seen.

A guy he didn't know eyed him from a partially open door at the top of the stairs. Chase had hoped Wade would greet him.

"How's it goin'?" Chase asked, smiling as he reached the top landing.

In response, the guy opened the door wider to admit him, but still did not reveal much of his body. Once he closed the door behind him, everything became clear.

The doorman was naked. He was an average-looking sort, skinny and tall, with salt-and-pepper hair and a matching beard, kind of a poor man's Mike. He had a little pot belly and a tribal tattoo that ran just under his collarbone. His dick stood at half-mast, and even in the light from the flickering candles, Chase saw that it was slick with spit or lube. Chase did not feel ready to investigate further.

"How's it goin'?" Chase repeated, trying to ignore the big screen TV flickering with images of a full-blown man-on-man gangbang and the scene which mirrored it, on the floor, on the sheet-covered couch, even in the kitchen, upon a table Chase hoped was strong and that no one actually ate off of.

To answer Chase's question, the doorman moved toward a miniature snowdrift of loaded white trash bags and rooted around until he found one that wasn't filled. He handed it to Chase, saying, "You can put your clothes in here. There's a marker over there somewhere if you wanna put your name on the bag." He smiled and, for a moment, Chase could almost believe he was at a regular party, you know, one where you didn't disrobe thirty seconds after walking through the front door.

Chase watched him wander back into the crowd of naked bodies. Within a minute, or maybe even less, a young Asian guy, looking no more than eighteen, positioned himself in front of Chase's new buddy and bent over. The salt-and-pepper guy quickly started fucking him.

*How romantic!*

There wasn't a condom in sight, at least not for that pair.

Chase hesitated.

*Maybe this is a little more hardcore than I realized it would be, especially if everyone's going bareback.* Chase, at least before he met Toby, had always been extra careful, sometimes even double-wrapping himself before fucking a guy. These days, he knew things were different, what with PREP drugs that held the HIV virus at bay— most of the time. Still, those drugs had no effect on other bugs like chlamydia, gonorrhea, herpes, hepatitis, or god knew what else. He was growing more and more uneasy by the minute, truly torn. His libido, stimulated by the porn and live sex shows all around, urged him to get naked and get busy. *Drop those inhibitions, mister, along with your pants.*

He leaned against the closed front door, allowing his gaze to roam over the large living room and its mix of naked bodies, varying in size, shape, and color, but all engaged in sucking, fucking, or at the very least, fondling and kissing. He spied a big punch bowl on the coffee table, and it was filled with an assortment of condoms, so that gave him a little relief. Next to the bowl were a couple bottles of lube, a jumbo can of Crisco, and a roll of paper towels. *They've thought of everything!* Chase giggled at this last thought. *Wade is truly the hostess with the mostess.*

"Dive in, buddy, the water's fine!" A redhead with a goatee and a snake tattoo encircling his left bicep shouted at him from across the room.

Chase smiled sheepishly back, thinking this had to be the only kind of situation where one would feel more awkward being clothed in a room full of strangers, rather than naked. The redhead had two guys kneeling at his feet and they were taking turns sucking him. One stopped and moved around behind the redhead, burying his face in his ass.

Chase had a vague feeling of nausea and of apprehension.

His dick was also rock hard. *Maybe the dick is the barometer of my true feelings*, Chase mused.

At last, he pulled off his sweatshirt, wondering where Wade was. He scanned the room once more, taking in the various and varied couplings, triplings, and more, searching for Wade's long dark mop of wavy hair.

No, he was not the guy with his legs in the air on the couch, getting fucked ruthlessly by a black guy. The dark skin on light skin was kind of beautiful, Chase reasoned, trying not to titter uncontrollably at the sighs and shrieks coming out of the guy getting fucked. *Is he enjoying himself? Or is he in horrible pain? Beats the hell out of me. In any event, he's not telling his fucker to stop or slow down, so I'll go with he's enjoying himself.*

Nor was Wade the blond twink, bent over the other end of the couch, while a shadowy figure kneeled behind him, pulling his ass cheeks apart and burying his face in the crack.

Nor was he the fish belly white fat guy in the corner, mouth open, and beating his meat. Chase dropped his sweatshirt to the floor, but left his jeans and shoes on as he wandered out to the kitchen. A guy took his mouth off another man's dick long enough to hiss, "No clothes, man. No clothes," as Chase passed by.

Chase ignored him.

In the kitchen, he saw more fully what he had only glimpsed. A handsome, all-American sort who looked to be in his early twenties lay spread-eagled across the kitchen table, his ass at the edge. He was grunting as a muscular older man who looked to be about fifty, with a shaved head and a well-trimmed beard, slammed into him, pulling his cock almost all the way out and then ramming it back in with a vengeance. From what he could see of it, the cock looked to be at least ten inches. The boy on the table seemed to be enjoying it. When he wasn't grunting or whimpering, he was encouraging the guy with words like, "Yeah, that's it. Fuck me hard, Daddy. Nail that ass."

Chase felt he had been transported into a Treasure Island Media porno. About six other guys stood around the table, watching, beating their own dicks and, Chase supposed, waiting for their turn.

He had a feeling the young man on the table wasn't too picky. As Chase left the room, he watched the younger guy take a hit of poppers, wiggle down further on the daddy's dick and cry out, "Come on, man, give me that load! Breed me!"

Chase shook his head and returned to the living room where, like a game of musical chairs, most everyone had rotated to a different partner and subtly shifted positions. If it was Treasure Island Media porn in the kitchen, the living room was Fellini debauchery. The room reeked of sweat, come, and poppers.

Chase headed down a dark hallway off the living room. He could see flickering light at the end of the hall, where a door stood open. Shadows passed in the half-light and Chase guessed this was where Wade's bedroom was. He had to be here somewhere.

Chase heard whimpers as he neared the room. He crept inside and joined another crowd of meat-beating onlookers. The centerpiece of the room was a metal-framed four-poster bed. Attached to the frame were chains and a leather sling.

And there was Wade, ankles up and in the stirrups, hanging in the sling, suspended a foot or so above the bed proper. A man with an average, but very hairy body and wearing a leather hood, stood at the foot of the bed, with his hand and part of his arm buried up Wade's ass. A can of Crisco was on the floor; someone had placed a roll of paper towels thoughtfully next to it. *Neat freak. Wade remembers everything. Was there some sort of guide for these gatherings? A Miss Manners for pigs?*

Chase stared at the scene, and as he did, Wade's somewhat glassy-eyed stare alit on him.

He said, "Hey Chase! Glad to see you made it." Chase was expecting some further instruction on what he should do now that he'd moved into these warm and somewhat murky waters. But all Wade did was ask, matter of factly, "Wanna fuck me?"

Chase smiled politely, shook his head, and turned away. "Maybe later." He ducked out of the room and doubted if he was missed.

He stood by the front door, struggling back into his sweatshirt. Single now or not, horny or not, this wasn't the scene for him.

For one, it was unsafe, completely so, regardless of the availability of condoms of if some of the revelers were on PREP. He felt really uncomfortable, and he was certain that discomfort could be driven away by drugs, crystal or coke, which he bet wouldn't be too hard to find at this soiree. Hell, probably many of these guys were already partying and that's why the scene was like something out of Hieronymus Bosch. *Misery may love company. Lust certainly does. But this kind of company? Not for me.*

*Call me old-fashioned, but I like to exchange a few words with a guy before I have sex with him.* He paused to look one last time at the room, where guys were fucking and sucking like crazy, but where it was also strangely quiet, and thought he had no judgment for these guys. If this is what got them off, then so be it.

It all seemed so empty to Chase and it bordered on sad.

He didn't find the scene hot. In fact, his hard-on had waned pretty quickly. Chase wasn't a prude, but he was old-fashioned, he supposed. He liked a little more intimacy with his sex. These guys? From his point of view, they were nothing more than a collection of orifices waiting to be filled or dicks desperate to fill something, someone...anyone. It seemed kind of lonely, really. Desperate. Did these guys get together on any kind of social basis when their erections waned? When fluids had been swapped? Or did they head out and, later, if they passed one another on the street, not pause in recognition?

He quickly opened the door, headed out, and closed it softly behind him. Again, he had the feeling not one person remarked on his leaving. Not one would wonder where he'd gone. And certainly no one would question why he didn't take the time to say goodbye. He even doubted anyone would even remember he was there the next day.

And that was okay. Guys like those at the party would never be people he'd hang out with.

Outside, the Ravenswood neighborhood had grown quieter and the night air chillier. The sky was completely dark now, its navy broken up by the sodium vapor of streetlamps. Noise pollution blocked out the stars and, Chase supposed, the moon too. A couple taxis passed him, a beat-up Ford 150 with a loud muffler, but other than vehicles, the streets were now empty. It felt as though everyone in the world had gone to bed.

Or was attending a sex party.

Chase at last felt liberated, like he could breathe once more. "We'd laugh about this, you and me," he whispered to Toby, suddenly feeling his presence alongside him. That feeling, or notion, wasn't absurd, nor was it scary.

It was a comfort.

"You don't think less of me for trying out that scene, do you? I mean, you and me, we watched porn together sometimes that depicted parties like that, but I know we both agreed it wasn't for us."

And it wasn't. It really wasn't. They'd been happy—complete unto each other. There was no need for fireworks, thrills, and chills. Although, while they were together, there were plenty of those. But their relationship's quality could also be measured by its comfortable silences, its lack of pressure, and its joy that came from just being near the other.

He hadn't worn a watch and wondered what time it was. Judging from the quiet all around, it was probably now in the wee hours of the morning.

He thought of Mike; had he made it home yet? Would he make it home at all tonight? Or was he at another party like the one Chase had just left?

He had the feeling Mike would have enjoyed the party he'd just left. Mike was more uninhibited and freewheeling. He was a good person, though. And Chase conceded there may have been another Mike, or two, or three, at the party. *You shouldn't be so quick to judge.*

He headed west on Wilson, back toward Western and the L station. It took him no time to reach it. The lights of Western Avenue stop called to him and, when he looked up, the station appeared deserted.

He missed Toby.

He missed Saturday nights in front of the TV, streaming something on Netflix or Hulu, maybe polishing off a bottle of wine before falling asleep wrapped in each other's arms.

"Those were the days, weren't they? I didn't have a clue they'd end so soon. Otherwise, I would have hung on tighter." Chase smiled sadly and pulled open the door to the station.

# Chapter Twelve

Chase spent the night on Mike's pullout couch doing little more than tossing and turning. Sleep was elusive. He drifted in and out of dreams, sometimes not sure if he was awake or asleep.

Images from the sex party stuck with him, whether he wanted them to or not. He vacillated between being turned on by what he had witnessed that night and being repelled.

When he did sleep, he dreamed of Toby. These dream visitations were always welcome—they were a way to be with Toby once more. But when Chase would wake, the ache of loss was that much more acute.

Or he'd wake, and the dream images would disperse: almost as though they were fleeing his conscious mind, teasing him and giving him a mysterious taste of what would never be again.

Toward morning, when the room was filled with a pale-gray light, one dream stuck to him with clarity. He was the one at the party being fucked on the kitchen table. He rolled his head from side to side and sucked in some air when he spied Toby standing in the corner and watching him along with the crowd that had gathered around.

Toby didn't look upset. In fact, a glimmer of a smile played about his lips and a mischievous light danced in his eyes. Chase recalled that one of his own hands, the one not pushing his top in deeper by pressing on his ass, lolled over the edge of the table. Toby stepped up and grabbed Chase's free hand, interlaced his fingers with Chase's, and squeezed.

The touch was electric.

That was when Chase woke, a sob caught on his lips, his dick hard and feeling like it was about to spurt. It was a strange combination of feelings—and potent. He turned on his stomach and thrust against the thin mattress, but it was no good.

He rolled back over to his side, letting his hand dangle off the edge of the sofa bed. "Oh Toby," he whimpered. "Why?"

Silently, he got up and went into the bathroom, taking his toothbrush with him. He splashed some water on his face, ran his wet fingers through his hair, and brushed his teeth. He eyed himself in the mirror. He had bags under his eyes and he looked older than his years but was otherwise presentable. "Good enough, anyway," he whispered to his reflection.

He returned to the office, quietly dressed in a pair of jeans, a T-shirt, fleece, and running shoes. He threw his remaining clothes into a duffel bag and glanced around one final time to ensure he wasn't leaving anything behind.

He sat at Mike's desk and pulled a sheet of paper from his printer. After finding a pen in one of the drawers, he pondered what to write, wondering if Mike had even returned home yet. It didn't seem like it. The condo was still, having that certain air of emptiness.

What should he say? He didn't want to appear ungrateful or unkind. Yet he wanted his message to be clear, with no room for misinterpretation. At last, he settled on simple.

*Dear Mike,*

*I know you might be a little surprised to find me gone, but I thought it was best that I head out to the airport early, see if I could get on standby for the next Seattle-bound flight.*

*As much as I appreciate your hospitality and friendship, I realized I wasn't ready for a weekend like this. Not. At. All.*

*All the hot men and sex...wow. Another time, another me, might have really gotten off on all this weekend offered. But there's a big part of me that's just kind of sad at seeing and experiencing all I have over the past few days. And it's only made me miss Toby more. Sorry to be such a sad sack.*

*I know. I know. I need to move on. No one gets that more than I do. At the same time, moving on feels like letting go of Toby, and that's something I never, ever want to do.*

*I also don't want you to think I'm being Mary Poppins and going judgmental on you. That's not it at all. You've always been a free spirit, living a life without hesitation or apology. And I admire that. I really do.*

*I'm just not ready.*

*I don't know if I'll ever be.*

*See, when you actually find real love...*

And Chase stopped writing; he didn't want this to become a sermon. The words, about finding real love and how unfulfilling casual sex could be after that, might just seem cruel to Mike...preachy. He went back and scratched out the last line. He stared down at the paper for a few minutes and just left it at:

*Thanks for everything. I'll be in touch.*

*Much love, Chase.*

He placed the sheet of paper over the computer keyboard, quickly pulled the sheets and pillows from the sofa bed and folded the mattress slowly back into the couch frame so it wouldn't make too much noise, just in case he was wrong and Mike was actually there, slumbering in his room.

The room looked almost as if no one had ever stayed there. Chase was both relieved and sad that his presence made so little difference. He choked back a sob as it came home to him how desperately alone he was. He had no idea what the cure for it was. Time?

The day had brightened more as he prepared to leave, and the condo remained still as Chase crept to the door, both his duffel and backpack slung over his shoulder. He heard the rumble of the L a few blocks over, sounding like the grumbling of a beast. Chase didn't know if he was up for sharing public transportation today.

*Maybe I should splurge for a cab or at least an Uber?*

*Come on! Get serious. There's no need for extravagance, especially since I have no idea how long I might have to camp out at O'Hare. Hell, they might not even have a flight to Seattle available today for me at all.*

He had his hand on the doorknob when Mike's voice, coming from behind, startled him. "And where do you think you're going, Miss?" There was laughter.

Chase turned around. He felt caught and heat rose to his face. He couldn't help but laugh at Mike calling him "Miss." Camp was just something Mike didn't do well.

But his question was a valid one. Mike leaned against the breakfast bar, wearing only a pair of boxer shorts, and crossed his arms over his chest. In spite of the "Miss," there was a mixture of curiosity and hurt on his face. His head was cocked as he waited for Chase's answer. "I assume you're not ducking out for coffee or even for a run along the lakefront. Not with that bag attached to your hand."

Chase swallowed, suddenly finding his mouth lacked spit. He scratched the back of his neck absently. What was he doing? Was this really the way to go about things? The heat in his cheeks intensified because he was ashamed at how cowardly he was acting. Chase grinned sheepishly. "I just thought..." Chase's voice trailed off as Mike cocked his head.

"You just thought what? That you'd creep out of here without saying goodbye? Without a word of thanks?"

"I left you a note," Chase said, sounding lame, sounding weak.

Mike went on. "I, at least, was looking forward to spending a week with you. I don't get it, man." Mike's words were tinged with anger and hurt.

Chase didn't blame him.

"It's not like that." Chase whined and stared down at the floor. "Can we sit?"

They both crossed the room. Mike took the couch, and Chase headed for a chair across from him, then reconsidered and sat next to him on the couch. After several minutes passed, Chase met Mike's stare. He drew in a deep breath, ready to talk, to try to explain himself, except he knew there was no explanation that could excuse his bad manners. He had to try anyway. "I'm sorry, Mike. I was going about this all the wrong way."

Mike's lips set in a line; he nodded. "Okay."

"But I don't know how to explain it." Chase pulled a pillow to his stomach, toyed with a stray thread at its corner. He blew out a sigh. "That's not true." He came to a decision. "Last night, I didn't stay home."

"I know."

Chase looked at Mike, surprised. "You do?"

"Yeah. I got home probably not long after you left. I thought we'd order a stuffed pizza from Giordano's, have a few beers. Quiet evening at home." He smiled and there was such kindness in his face.

*Why am I such a fool?* "Oh."

"So what did you do?"

Now, Chase wasn't sure he should say. But as he thought last night before going into Wade's apartment— *in for a penny, in for a pound.* He let it all out in a guilt-laden rush of air. "I went to a sex party."

Mike thought about the new information for a minute and then smiled his lopsided grin. "Good for you, buddy." Mike punched his arm.

"No. You're wrong there. It wasn't good for me." Chase flashed on the decadent images from the night before. "Not at all. It wasn't even right for me." Chase put the pillow back in its place on the end of the couch. "It was, in fact, terrible. Empty. I can't remember a time when I felt more out of place. I ended up just feeling lost, sad, and alone." Chase turned a little more to Mike. "It made me miss Toby more, not less. Hot as that scene might have been to imagine, it couldn't compare to a night at home with him, ordering in Chinese food and watching the latest stand-up special from Hannah Gadsby. Or even bingeing on some old sitcom like *Golden Girls* or *Seinfeld*." How he longed for those simple pleasures! Chase drew in some more breath, surprised that it actually helped he was talking about this. "I know that probably doesn't make any sense to you. Or you think I have to be the most boring gay man on the planet."

Mike leaned forward and gathered Chase in his arms, pulling him close, rubbing the hair at the back of his head. "I don't think that. And I do understand. That's why I didn't stay out too long last night. I figured you'd be here, sad. But I also just preferred spending the evening with you. It's been so long since you've been back."

Chase moved back a little so he could look up at Mike. There was something he couldn't read in his friend's expression—sadness maybe? Who knew?

"Listen. We can talk more about everything, if you'd just stay. Please, Chase. Maybe this is my fault, with all the IML crap. I should have been more sensitive and played things low key. Sometimes, I can be dense. But I get it. And we can do quiet, easy. Okay?"

"Aw, Mike, I don't know. This weekend, IML, all this free-flowing sex. As I said, it's just not for me. Not right now, anyway."

"I just told you, man, we don't have to go back to IML. I don't even want to! Honestly, I've been so many times, missing more of this year's festivities certainly won't kill me." He laughed softly. "We don't have to go the leather ball tonight, or any of the parties, or the crowded bars."

"Are you sure you don't want to miss out?" Chase remembered how long Mike used to look forward to IML when he and Toby lived in Chicago, remembered his unrepentant tomcat ways.

"Chase, honey, I'm not missing anything. What I *would* miss is having my old friend here with me. *You* mean more to me than any of those things. I'm glad I caught you sneaking out. If I'd woken up and you were really and truly gone, I'd have been crushed."

"Really?"

"Of course. Don't be stupid." Mike looked away, disengaged from holding Chase and stood. He walked to the window and looked out. Then he turned back to Chase. "Listen, I had a surprise planned for us for later this week. We can just move it up. No problem."

"What do you mean?" Chase asked. "You've done more than enough."

"Well, I wanted to spring it on you, a prize for coming clear across the country to hang out with me. But the cat's out of the bag. See, Mom and Dad are still down in Arizona, and their place up at Lake Geneva is sitting there empty."

Chase recalled Mike's parents' "cabin" on the lake in Wisconsin in the little town of Fontana. Cabin was really a too-humble word for a three-bedroom fieldstone house with stunning water views. An expansive lush green lawn led down to the family boat dock, where a small power boat was moored.

Mike continued. "I wanted to wait until the leather festivities were over, then I thought you and I could head up there for the rest of your time here. Really relax, maybe take the boat out, eat some walleye and ice cream, drink some Leinenkugel's. We could lay on the dock all day and get sunburnt, watch the water skiers." Mike scooted over closer to Chase, so that their shoulders touched. "I can forego the rest of the IML weekend. In fact, I wouldn't miss it, really. It's getting a little old."

"Oh shut it. You love IML." Chase shook his head.

Mike grinned, but he shook his head. "So what do you say you forget whatever silly idea was running through your head earlier this morning? Just let it go, man. Stick to your original plan. Go take a shower, and I'll whip us up some bacon, eggs, and coffee, okay? Sound good? Once we stuff ourselves, we'll get in the car and head north." Mike glanced out the window once more. "It looks like it's gonna be a gorgeous day. Plenty of sunshine and my weather app tells me it's gonna get unseasonably warm. First time in years it hasn't rained on Memorial Day." He chuckled.

Chase grinned and surprised himself—he actually felt the relaxation begin to flow through him as though it had been injected directly into his veins. He couldn't imagine a nicer scenario. He could practically see the sun shimmering on Lake Geneva, its serene surface dotted by sailboats and small power craft.

"Yeah. I could use a shower. If you don't mind."

"Mind? Honey, take a whiff of yourself." Mike waved a hand in front of his face and cracked up, doubling over.

Chase rolled his eyes. He finally returned the punch to the arm Mike had given him earlier. "Fucker."

"Go take your shower. Breakfast will be up by the time you're done. Scrambled?"

# Chapter Thirteen

Once they were outside Chicago and its sprawl of northern suburbs, the scenery out Mike's Jeep window got dull fast. Chase looked out at things that could have been anywhere: McDonald's, Walmarts, and strip malls, dotted here and there with small-town restaurants and chain gas stations. The monotony of the American landscape was broken up with farmlands, billboards, and copses of trees that had not yet been felled for even more development.

Traffic was fairly light as they headed north, the Jeep's radio tuned to WXRT, a mishmash of DJ chatter and alternative music that Chase barely heard. Mike remarked that the traffic was light because everyone, on this late Sunday morning, was probably already at their holiday weekend destination. "If we come home on Monday, buddy, you'll see *traffic*."

To pass the time, Chase brought out his phone. "You ever stumble across this blog? *Tales from the Sexual Underground*? It's hilarious."

Mike shook his head without removing his gaze from the road. Chase was surprised; the blog seemed right up Mike's alley. He would have expected him to be a fan.

"Sounds like a good title for my autobiography, don't you think?" He didn't laugh, as Chase imagined. His expression, behind mirror aviator sunglasses, was inscrutable.

Chase didn't answer. He found the blog and scrolled through the posts until he found one that made him snicker. He'd read it before and it was just so, so sick that it made him break out in hoots of highly uncomfortable laughter, but laughter nonetheless.

"Now keep your eyes on the road while I read." And he began:

## "Big and Sexy: A Late-Night Tale"

It was 4:00 a.m. There was no one in the supermarket other than my pal Pete Thickwhistle, an old woman who smelled of camphorated oil, feeling up the cucumbers, and a couple of delicious Hispanic stock boys. These, and a bored-looking, gum-cracking cashier with nothing to do, comprised the entire supermarket population that hot summer night.

Pete, who had suffered from insomnia for years (probably because he had trained himself to stay up all night listening for sounds of his parents' squeaking mattress, which came regularly twice a week and afforded Pete a kind of queasy arousal), thought that the late hour and the warm night had conspired together to create the perfect grocery shopping opportunity: no long lines, and gloriously empty aisles which he could peruse at his utmost leisure.

But the hot August night had also ignited another desire in Pete: namely, to fill more than his larder. Yes, boys and girls, our friend was horny. And as the "total bottom" he described himself to patrons of various watering holes around town, as well as in personal profiles on Scruff and Grindr, Pete needed to have that wonderful feeling of rectal fullness not offered by something so common as a bowel movement.

After shamelessly cruising the Hispanic stock boys for what seemed like more than an hour, Pete despaired, thinking the supermarket was going to offer him no succor other than of the gastronomical variety. Damn! It was hot; Pete was desperate; and every bar in town was now closed. Even the chat rooms and hookup sites were dead, or dying, at this late, twilight hour. On them, Pete knew he'd only find two types of men—the very desperate and tweakers.

That was when Pete met his salvation…or his downfall. Who would have thought that a saunter down the hair care products aisle would offer such temptation to a horny young man, looking to get himself stuffed like a Thanksgiving turkey? But there it was, prominent on the shelf of hair sprays, along with the Aqua Nets, and the White Rains: a can of "Big and Sexy" hairspray. Big and Sexy was just what Pete wanted, and the simple words ignited a firestorm of misplaced desire. Pete wasted no time: he hurried down the aisle, looking for a suitable lubricant when he came across a lowly bottle of Suave hand cream (unscented, but Pete would soon put that to right!!).

Hell, Pete thought, who's around to see? And this will take but a few minutes. So he dropped his drawers right there in the hair care aisle, reached for the can of Big and Sexy with a trembling paw, slathered it up with Suave, took a deep cleansing breath, and slowly slid it into his hungry hole. The feeling, while not equal to that of upstairs neighbor Ramon's beer-can penis, was pretty close to heaven. That is, until Pete stiffened at the sound of a deep bass voice behind him.

"And what do you think you're doing, miss?" The big, black security guard had appeared out of nowhere. Under other circumstances, Pete would have been thrilled with the specter of this handsome morsel of masculinity. But not tonight. Tonight, he only felt a sense of fear and something else that went far beyond mere embarrassment.

Pete yanked the can quickly from himself, groaning. On account of its slipperiness, it clattered to the floor, where Pete was humiliated to see obvious signs of recent anal penetration obscuring the Big and Sexy trademark.

Red-faced, he turned to the security officer, tugging his khakis back up. "I...I was horny—" Pete tried to explain with a sheepish grin. "—and I didn't see any signs prohibiting what I was doing."

"Tell it to the judge, Mary," the security officer said.

And that's exactly what Pete did, one month later, down at the circuit court at Belmont and Western.

After the helpless laughter that brought both of them to tears, Chase and Mike finally grew quiet, saying little for the remainder of the trip. What, after all, does one say to hearing about such exploits, beyond hoping they were a figment of the author's very twisted imagination and sense of humor?

As they were getting close to Mike's parents' place in Fontana, Mike turned the radio down. "Okay, I wasn't gonna ask because the shame is wafting off you like BO, but I can't resist."

"What?"

"Tell me about this sex party. Or don't—if it makes you uncomfortable."

"Well, it doesn't make me as uncomfortable as picturing what I just read to you, so I guess I can talk about it." Chase began describing his previous night, going through the various couplings he had witnessed, the great bodies and the not-so-great ones. "The weird thing is how quiet it was." Chase shrugged. "I dunno. I might have stayed if someone had just taken a minute out to talk to me a little, you know?"

Mike took his eyes off the road for a minute to give Chase an evil grin. "Sweetie, people are not there to exchange prize-winning peach cobbler recipes or shoot the shit about who's going to be a finalist on *Dancing with the Stars*."

"I know *that*." Chase laughed, feeling surprisingly a little self-conscious. "But that's just the problem, for me anyway. I may be getting old, but the whole casual sex routine just doesn't do it for me anymore. I mean, I got hard looking at these guys fucking and sucking, eating butt. It was hot, you know. But then, it wasn't.

"I guess what Toby and I had kind of erased the charm of scenes like last night." Chase grew quiet for several minutes. "You do that kind of stuff, right? The sex parties? No judgment here. But does it ever get old for you?"

Mike smiled, but he stared out the window for the longest time, not saying anything. Chase must have hit a nerve, and he anticipated what Mike's response might be.

At last, Mike spoke without glancing over at Chase. "Oh yeah, I've done my share of sex parties, bathhouses, back rooms, one-nighters." He shrugged. "No regrets here. But maybe, like you, I'm tiring of the scene, as one might say."

"You don't have to say that to make me feel better."

"No. No, I'm not. Last night was a good example. I went out to the Cell Block, had a couple beers, got called "sir" by more than a few hot boys, one of whom even offered to bring me back to his apartment on Cornelia where he'd do whatever I wanted." Mike stared out the window for a while, made a turn on a more rural road with a simple letter for a name. "But all I really wanted to do was go home."

"Did you?"

Mike laughed. "Old habits die hard, my friend. No, Mikey wandered into the backroom, which was packed. It was dark, some guy was wandering around completely naked, with a pair of shackles around his ankles making him hobble. Little groups stood in the corners and along the walls, guys sucking each other off, stroking, kissing. One guy was getting fucked while a bunch stood around watching. I got horned up, let some guy blow me. It took all of a couple minutes, especially with a bottle of poppers shoved under my nose by yet another stranger."

"Yeah?"

"Yeah. And if I passed him on the street today, I couldn't tell you who he was. I doubt that I could pick him out of a lineup. I don't know the color of his hair or even, really, the color of his skin. It was too dark. He could have been anyone for all I know." Mike looked at Chase. "Just like you did last night, I felt kind of empty once I shot my load. All I wanted to do was get the hell out of there. What does that say about pleasure? What does that say about *me?*" Mike drew in a deep breath, releasing it in a long sigh. And then he asked something that surprised Chase. "You know that old Peggy Lee song, 'Is That All There Is?'"

"Oh yeah. Of course. It's a classic."

"Well, that's how I felt. I put my dick back in my pants, zipped up, set a nearly full can of beer back on the bar, and got the fuck out of there." He paused and Chase could see him remembering the night in all its glory, or lack of it.

Mike continued, "I was really hoping you'd be home when I got back. But then I saw that you'd gotten the energy up to go out. And that made me smile. I was glad for you." He looked over at Chase at last. "Sorry it didn't turn out better. Sorry no one talked to you. But the guys at that party?"

"Yeah?"

"If you don't know it, I'll let you in on a little secret. I'd bet my life savings that most, if not all of them, were hopped up on Tina and couldn't think of anything other than getting their holes filled. Wouldn't matter who was doing the filling, as long as Miss Tina was calling the shots."

Tina, or crystal meth, had come along in a big way after Chase and Toby had become a couple. Of course, Chase had heard of the drug and how prevalent it had become in the gay community, but he had never tried it. "You ever done it?"

"What, Tina? Sure. It's hard to be much of a sex pig these days without running into her. I did my dance with her, the sick bitch. Enough was never enough. Thank god, I pulled away from *that* scene before Miss Tina got her claws in me too deep." Mike's features grew dark. "It's all in the past now. With Tina, you get over her or you get dead. There's no 'recreational use' of that stuff. Toxic. It corrodes your soul."

"Wow," Chase said. "I had no idea." He touched Mike's leg for a minute. "I'm glad you made it out of there alive."

"Oh me too, buddy. Me too. Look, we're here."

The view silenced them both, even though Chase knew it had to have been very familiar to Mike. Before them spread the lake, in all its azure beauty, the sunlight reflected on its shifting waters like gems. Around the perimeter of the lake, small tree-covered hills rose up, green. And above them, the sky, a wide-open expanse, was dotted with a few strands of clouds that did nothing to hide the golden brilliance of the sun.

What he was seeing caused Chase to breathe a little slower. He could actually feel his heart rate and respiration drop to a more relaxed tempo. A small feeling of joy rose up inside him, inspired by childlike wonder at all that open sky and water. He wanted, like a boy, to get out of the car, strip off his clothes, run across the lawn, hop onto the white-painted boat dock and dive off its end. Then, he could swim out to the blue-painted raft bobbing in the water and just lie there, letting the sun bake him while he gazed up at passing clouds, imagining the shapes they made.

"No matter how many times I turn in this drive, the view never fails to take my breath away," Mike said. And, as though reading Chase's mind, he continued, "Makes me feel like a kid again, seeing that."

Chase grinned. "I'm so glad we came up here. I didn't realize it until I laid eyes on it, but this, I think was exactly what I needed. It soothes me; it really does. Thanks, Mike."

Mike waved away his gratitude. "Thank you for coming with me. We're gonna have a great time—free and easy. No commitments. No pressure."

They continued down the long drive that led to the gorgeous fieldstone house that almost seemed to rise organically from the well-manicured and almost surreal green lawn and shrubbery. The windows reflected the sky. The house and the lake seemed worlds away from what they had left in Chicago.

And that was a very good thing indeed.

Chase took it all in as they cruised up to the house parking under a portico at the side of the house.

*

Once inside, with bags put away, Chase sat down in the large pit group and looked out through the floor-to-ceiling windows facing the lake. Things couldn't have been more perfect. This was escapism at its finest.

Chase had grown up in pretty low-income circumstances. He'd never describe his family as poor because, as his mother always told him, "We don't have much, but we always have enough." Still, growing up, Chase's idea of a vacation was visiting his Aunt Marcy and Uncle Steve's lakeside cabin, which was so primitive it didn't even have a bathroom. You used the outhouse and grabbed a bar of soap to bathe in the lake. Chase smiled at the memory, though. The cabin couldn't hold a candle to this kind of luxury, but they still held some of the happiest memories of his boyhood.

Outside everything looked freshly washed and new, the colors vibrant. The colors were deeply saturated and it occurred to Chase that if he took a picture right now and posted it on social media, he'd be accused of using filters to get the effect.

But a picture really couldn't do this beauty justice. And he wouldn't be posting anything on social media, anyway. He'd stopped Facebook and Twitter shortly after losing Toby. There had actually been too many condolences, too much sympathy. Every time he went online, the well-intentioned kindness of friends and followers ripped the scab off the wound of his grief.

*

They'd had lunch—ham and Swiss sandwiches on rye and potato salad, washed down with beer that Mike picked up at a little deli in Fontana on the way.

The siren call of the shimmering lake had proved almost irresistible. Chase had rushed down to the water, stuck a foot in, screamed, and turned back to Mike, laughing. "That's fuckin' cold." And Mike had told him they'd have to come back in late July or August for good swimming.

Since the water had been too cold for swimming, Chase and Mike had spent the day tooling around the lake in Mike's dad's motorboat, taking in all the gorgeous homes and mansions that lined the lake's shores. When they docked, they lay out on the white painted dock that fronted the house, both getting a little sunburned. They didn't do much talking, simply enjoying the cool breezes off the water, the heat of the sun on their bodies, and the music coming out of Mike's Bluetooth speaker, the bluesy wail of Koko Taylor their accompaniment. Mike loved the blues singer and had seen her many times in Chicago before she'd passed away in 2009.

They went through more than a couple bottles of Leinenkugels, the local favorite. The combination of cold beer and warm sun was soporific and Chase fought to keep his eyes open. He didn't want to ruin his time here with a bad burn. And, in spite of the No-Ad oil he lathered on himself, he knew he'd been a little reddened come evening, because the suntan oil only had a protection factor of four. He shrugged and grabbed another beer from the cooler. A bit of a sunburn was a small price to pay for this peace and relaxation.

The music shifted from Koko Taylor to BB King. "This is heaven," Chase sighed.

Mike said nothing, but reached over and touched his arm in agreement.

*

Because Mike's family had been coming to Lake Geneva for years (the house had been passed down through a couple of generations), Mike knew a lot of people who made their living from the tourist trade and one of them was Pete Mulligan, the maître d' of Mise En Place, a little French bistro on the main street in the town of Lake Geneva. The place had only about a dozen tables and the holiday weekend was, predictably, totally booked.

But Mike was able to get them in. "Hey, tricking around half your adult life has its benefits," he explained to Chase as they were getting dressed for dinner.

"Half? Just half?" Chase wondered.

Mike ignored him. "Pete and I used to fuck the summers away back when we were in college and both of us were up here with our families. That boy was an insatiable bottom! He's a hot guy, you'll see, but now he's totally devoted to this Andre character who owns the restaurant. They've been together for, like, ten years now." Mike sighed. "But Pete and I have stayed good buddies, so he was able to squeeze us in."

Mention of a happy couple was a bittersweet reminder of what Chase had lost. *Will it always be this way?*

The restaurant, Chase was pleased to see when they entered, was unlike anything he would have expected up here at the lake. Most of the restaurants he remembered from coming up with Mike and on other trips, specialized in burgers and fish and chips and the clientele wore flip-flops, T-shirts, shorts, and the occasional swimming suit.

But Mise En Place was charming, looking as though it had been lifted straight from the Left Bank in Paris. A simple black-and-white tile floor, stamped-tin ceiling, and pale-salmon walls made the place look homey and inviting, unpretentious. The few tables were covered with white linen tablecloths and each sported a different size and colored vase filled with spring wildflowers. A chalkboard hanging on the wall announced the evening's specials.

"This is really something," Chase said as Pete led them to their table.

"Wait until you taste the food. The steak frites are to die for. And the mussels!" Mike enthused. "Make sure if you get them, you order extra bread to sop up the white wine and garlic they're steamed in."

Pete pulled out their chairs for them. He was a gorgeous man, in a Slavic sort of way, with pale, almost-white blond hair streaked through with gold, deep-brown eyes, full lips, and an amazing tan that spoke of a person who worked nights. His shoulders were broad and his hips narrow. He was a true ten.

After Pete made brief chitchat and left them alone, Chase couldn't help asking Mike, "And you haven't gotten together with him since you were in college? How could you resist? My God, the man is a God, right here in Wisconsin!" Chase laughed.

Mike shook his head. "Oh, believe me, I've tried. But ever since he and Andre hooked up, the guy has been as faithful as can be; he simply will not stray, not even for the likes of me. Can you imagine?" Mike winked. "The closest I came was a passionate kiss one New Year's Eve when I was up here, but that's it." Mike looked wistful. "Those college days were beautiful, man. All that horniness and energy and that kid could take it like a champ. He could never get enough! That Andre must have a monster dick and the stamina to go with it to keep Pete so true blue."

"Okay, okay, down boy."

They looked over the wine list and settled on a bottle of Vouvray champagne to start. After they'd each had a glass, they ordered, starting with a simple field greens salad with hazelnuts and a lemony vinaigrette, and then steak frites for Mike and mussels for Chase.

They talked as they savored the perfectly prepared food, their eyes meeting above the flickering candlelight. They discussed the quality of the meat and seafood, the wine, the state of the economy, what their guilty TV pleasures were—Mike's was *Shameless* and Chase's, *The Sopranos*, which he was on his third go-round of viewing the entire opus of seasons. And even though he'd seen each episode enough times to have lines memorized, he was still stumped by the ending. They talked of who they thought should win the Oscar races that year. They waxed philosophic about their approaching middle ages, and Mike, ever the realist, pointed out that they were both already there and hardly "approaching." After they got their laughter under control, they shared memories of other summers on the lake.

Mike told Chase about the most incredible blowjob he had gotten in a service stairwell at IML, by an insatiable little twink who kept up eagerly with a line of men that only continued to grow. "That kid went home with a belly full of come!" Mike laughed.

"Yeah, and hopefully a prescription for penicillin."

"Ah, don't be such a Debbie Downer."

They talked about their jobs, and the reason Mike had never found the perfect guy to settle down with. It had always been a mystery to both Toby and Chase why Mike was perpetually single. He was a catch, indeed! But although lust always worked out for him, real love and intimacy never seemed to.

Chase wondered what his life would have been like if he had remained in Chicago instead of moving to Seattle. He compared Mise En Place with Bastille, his favorite French restaurant in Seattle.

They discussed many things, and by the time the dessert came, a couple of decadent, homemade chocolate truffles infused with chili pepper and a vanilla bean crème brûlée, Mike brought up something that, to him, was surprising and to Chase, miraculous and bittersweet.

As Mike licked a bit of custard from his lip, he reached out to cover Chase's hand across the table. Their plates were empty, the wine bottles—they had ordered a second—dead soldiers, and they had had a perfectly lovely time. Oblivion with French food, a handsome man, and a subdued setting was how Chase thought of it. And he was grateful.

"You know what?" Mike asked.

"What?"

"I don't mean to bring this wonderful evening down, and I hope you don't think I am, but I was kind of struck and surprised by something this evening."

"Oh?"

"Yeah, don't take this the wrong way, but we had quite the gabfest tonight."

"Who knew we could be such talkers?" Chase asked. He really meant it too. He was an avowed introvert and much preferred taking a back seat when it came to conversation. Listening was always his specialty, but tonight things were different. Maybe it was the wine that had loosened his tongue. Or the company.

Probably, it was both. It was liberating, in a way, to step away if only for a few moments, from the oppression of his grief. It had hung around his shoulders for so long, weighing him down, that he scarcely noticed it—until he was granted a reprieve and it was gone. Shame mixed in with his relief. *Will life ever feel normal again?*

"But there was one topic that, through all the stuff we talked about, didn't come up." Mike drained his wine glass. He gazed across the table at Chase. *And here it is...*

Chase felt a chill pass through him and he even shivered a bit. He knew where this was headed, and it didn't take him more than a second to make the connection. "Toby," he said softly.

Mike nodded. "I really don't mean to put a damper on the evening, but I think it's kind of important. It says something. And not necessarily something bad."

Chase stared down at the remains of the custard from the crème brûlée. He pushed a spoon around in the custard and broken sugar shell. Guilt rose in him. His shoulders slumped. The aftertaste of the wonderful dessert went dry in his mouth.

"Hey, I didn't mean to make you feel bad, Chase. I think it's a good thing. You've been so down, which of course is very understandable. I have too. But ever since you got to Chicago, it's like a cloud was hanging over you. Today on the boat and here tonight at dinner, it was like the old Chase had come back. You were animated, fun; you were enjoying yourself. You didn't know I was looking at you on the boat, but I was." Mike shook his head. "There was such a blissful look on your face. All the worry lines, and I was beginning to think those were permanent, were gone. There was just you, content, happy, your skin a little red from the sun, a little damp from the spray. You closed your eyes, and I think you were just savoring the moment." He squeezed Chase's hand. "And that was good to see."

Chase nodded. He felt he'd been thrown a bit of a reprieve. Still, he couldn't completely quell the guilt he felt at having forgotten, for a day and part of an evening, his Toby. But he wouldn't reveal those feelings to Mike, who seemed so pleased with his mood. So he just said, "You're right."

Chase understood what Mike had seen and why it was a small cause for celebration within his friend, yet this odd guilt, no less real even though it wasn't quite rational, continued to weigh him down. He wished Mike hadn't mentioned things. But could he ever really forget? Move on? Did he even want to?

Toby's face rose up in his mind's eye. Why couldn't it have been Toby on that boat with him, enjoying the sun and the water? He would have so loved it—he loved being on anything that floated. Back in Seattle, they'd sometimes simply take the ferry over to Bainbridge or Vashon Island and then back again, just for the trip across Puget Sound.

Chase's gaze flickered away; he traced the embroidery on the napkin. He didn't smile.

"Aw, come on now. We both miss Toby, but he loved life and he would want to see you having a good time."

Chase put on his best smile and tried to infuse his face with brightness, force a twinkle into his eye. But the fact that he had forgotten Toby for a couple of hours was like a stab to his heart, a reminder that as more and more time passed he might forget what his face looked like, what he ate for breakfast, who he *was*. And that was beyond sad.

The waiter brought their check, and Mike snatched it up. He didn't allow Chase any argument or protest. "This is my treat. I won't have it any other way."

As Chase was finishing up filling out the credit card receipt and signing, Pete stopped by the table to wish them a good night and to offer them an umbrella.

"It's raining?" Chase turned to peer out at the darkness pressing in on the front windows. "I hadn't even noticed."

Pete smiled. "You were distracted by this handsome lug across the table." He squeezed Mike's shoulder. "Yeah, it's pouring and they're predicting thunder, lightning, and high winds for overnight, so you boys should hurry right home."

Chase was stunned. He'd heard no thunder. And the day had been so perfectly sun-kissed that the notion of a storm didn't even enter his mind.

They refused the offer of the umbrella and dashed out into the night. Immediately, their clothes were soaked, plastered to their skin. Laughing and spitting water out, they reached the Jeep and rushed to scurry inside. The rain drummed down like a tribal beat on the vehicle's canvas top. Chase relaxed into the seat, closing his eyes. "There's nothing more soothing than the sound of rain beating down on a roof, is there? I could go to sleep right here."

Mike laughed. "I agree. But we can do better on the sleeping arrangements." He started the Jeep and pulled out, his tires hissing on the pavement, windshield wipers thumping back and forth.

"Thank you, Mike." Chase surprised himself and leaned over to plant a kiss on Mike's cheek.

Mike kept his eyes on the road.

*

The house was dark as they approached down the long drive. The rain had slowed to a steady downpour, quiet and almost soothing as they walked to the house. Since they were already soaked, there was no cause to rush. The air smelled newly washed—damp and fresh. Chase could even smell the damp earth, the wet grass. The clouds above them, dusky deep-blue shapes, parted to reveal a half moon and stars, so many stars. It was always amazing to see the stars once one got away from the city, which blocked their light. They twinkled like diamonds on a vast field of navy blue velvet.

The cold raindrops felt invigorating, which had heated up some under the influence of two bottles of Vouvray. Yet, even as they neared the back door, the rain was dissipating, slowing to nothing more than a light mist.

Mike fumbled with the keys, laughing as he dropped them before fitting the house key into the deadbolt on the heavy oak door. Inside, he groped for the light switch. "Huh," he said because when he flicked the switch, nothing happened. As if to explain, a bright flash of blue-white heat lightning lit up the room, followed by a clap of thunder.

"Power's out," he explained to Chase.

"Really? No. Really?" Chase laughed. "You should be some sort of detective." Chase glanced up at the sky. Yes, the stars and moon were present, but he had a feeling the storm clouds weren't quite finished with them yet. Across the black void of the lake, they massed on the horizon.

"Smart-ass." Mike closed the door and they made their way gingerly inside, lit by the dull gray coming in through the windows. Mike offered, "I'll light some candles. Let me just run down to the cellar to make sure a circuit breaker hasn't been tripped. I doubt that's it since it's pretty dark out there. No matter what time it is, you usually see a light coming from a window or two. While I'm there, I can grab us a new bottle of wine. You wouldn't believe the collection Dad has down there. It's probably worth a mint. But he does adore the stuff, so does Mom. You want another white?"

Chase shuddered a bit. He was already a little unsteady on his feet. "Oh man, I'm already pretty tipsy from dinner. I don't know." Even though he knew he'd had too much, one more glass surely couldn't hurt, could it?

"Yeah, you know. I can see it your wantin' eyes." Mike snapped his fingers. "It's decided. We're having another bottle. Let's switch regions. There's an amazing Pinot Grigio I'm pretty sure he bought a case of last year. Can't let it gather dust too long."

"I guess it wouldn't do any good to protest." Chase realized he wasn't about to protest, anyway.

"No good at all." Mike started cautiously toward the kitchen, where the door to the cellar was. He paused and looked back at Chase. "There are candles and matches in the sideboard over there by the windows. Why don't you take care of giving us a little illumination while I get the wine?"

"Okay, but how are you going to see anything downstairs?"

"Are you kidding? My dad is fanatical about things like flashlights and keeping the batteries fresh. There's one hanging at the top of the stairs. I'll be fine. And I'll be right back."

Chase busied himself finding and then setting out candles and holders. He placed them about the living room and lit each one with a disposable lighter he found in the drawer with the candles.

Outside, the rain changed its mind. Now it smeared the windows, making the view to the outside murky and obscured. The wind picked up its intensity and tempo. Every couple of minutes, the room lit up with an electric, almost pewter flash. Thunder shook the house. Chase found it a comfort and felt safe here inside.

The candles made the room feel like a sanctuary, shelter from the storm. Reverence in dim, flickering light.

Chase plopped down on the couch and waited for Mike to come back, watching the storm outside the windows, the way the rain pelted off the lake's surface when he viewed it during a flash of lightning. He could imagine closing his eyes and simply drifting off to sleep, right here on this soft leather nest.

He perked up when the sounds of Mike in the kitchen getting ice out of the freezer came to him. He sat up straighter, hearing the clink of the ice as Mike filled a bucket.

He thought about telling him not to bother, that he should keep the freezer and refrigerator doors shut. Who knew how long it would be before the power came back on? But in the end, he shrugged. Why did he always feel the need to be so practical? So what if a few things spoiled? At least their wine, tonight, would have a chill.

Mike returned to the room with two wineglasses in one hand and a bottle of wine in the other. With a pop, he uncorked the wine and filled the glasses. Then he plunged the bottle into the ice.

Making sure not to spill any wine, he made his way to the couch. He handed Chase a glass and then sat next to him. He raised his glass in a toast.

"To good friends. And good memories. And, of course, to Toby."

They clinked glasses. Chase felt a little shiver of want and nostalgia pass through him at the mention of Toby. He wondered if he were perhaps here with them tonight. And if he were, what did he think? Did he approve? Did he want to be with them, in the flesh? Chase wished they'd done this when Toby was alive. If only they could have one more chance! *We always think there's time to do everything when, in fact, the opposite is true.*

Mike glanced over at him. "You look sad."

Chase leaned a little toward him. "Not sad so much as—what's the word—feeling a little loss or lost."

"He's here," Mike said softly. "I can feel him all around us."

"I'm glad. I want him to be. I was just thinking I wish we'd done this kind of weekend before—the three of us, you know?"

"I know. But we can do it now, for him, for us." He raised his glass again and clicked it against Chase's. They sat in silence for a while, listening to the *thrum* of the rain on the roof.

Mike took a sip of his wine and set it on the coffee table.

Chase regarded him as though seeing him for the first time. His face, the olive complexion and the salt-and-pepper beard and hair, softened in the candlelight.

How had Chase never noticed how full Mike's lips were? How chiseled his features? He had always seen Mike almost as a brother, not someone for whom he'd feel any attraction. While he acknowledged how handsome and virile he was, he simply had never considered him in those terms.

Until now...

"You know what would be perfect?" Mike asked.

Chase shook his head and took another sip of the wine, which was good, crisp and chilled just the right amount. It lingered delightfully on his tongue for almost a full minute after swallowing. The taste was clean, fruity, but with no cloying aftertaste. He responded to Mike's question. "What?"

"A fire."

"It *is* kind of chilly in here."

"Yeah, I think the storm pushed the temperature outside down about twenty degrees."

Chase shrugged. "Need any help?"

"Nah. Dad has these special starter logs that will have things going in no time."

True to his word, Mike had the logs arranged and a cheerful fire burning in less than ten minutes.

He returned to the couch, smelling just slightly of wood smoke. It was how Chase might imagine the devil smelling.

"Thanks, this is nice," Chase said, scooting close to Mike. Without even thinking about what he was doing, he laid his head on Mike's shoulder. The gesture was neither awkward nor forced, only natural, as though it was next in a series of moves meant to comfort both of them.

Mike didn't say anything but slid his arm around Chase, leaning in closer so the full lengths of their bodies touched.

"If I didn't know better, all of this—the wine, the candlelight, the fire—I would say you were trying to seduce me, sir." Chase chuckled to show he was kidding. *But am I?*

Mike didn't say anything for a while. "Are you sure you do know better?" He turned to Chase and engaged his gaze. Mike's eyes were shimmering in the flickering light of the candles.

Chase didn't answer. Chase couldn't answer. Not really. He wasn't sure what the right words would be.

The two men stared into the fire for a long while. The only sounds were the steady beat of the rain on the roof and the cackle of flames in the fireplace. Chase felt like they were the only people in the world awake right now. No, that wasn't right. Chase felt like they were the only people in the world. Period.

It seemed only natural when at last Mike turned, lifted Chase's chin, and kissed him. The kiss was long, probing, and warm, the culmination of a very happy day spent together. Chase was aware that the wine and the dim light had relaxed him as he settled into the kiss, grabbing the back of Mike's neck to draw him closer, tasting the wine on his tongue. He let go, allowing himself to feel nothing but Mike's hard body pressed against his own and the pleasant rough of his beard on his face and neck.

He also couldn't ignore Mike's insistent hardness pressed into his thigh.

This felt good, he might have thought, if he was doing any conscious thinking; this is what he had hungered for: a human and a physical connection. He'd missed this so much, had almost given up on it.

After a moment, he pulled away and smiled at Mike, picked up his wine, and drank. He stared forward at the darkness pressing against the windows, as though wanting to come inside to seek shelter from the storm.

Mike started to say something, but Chase put a finger to his lips. Chase filled his mouth with wine, leaned forward, and transferred it into Mike's mouth, drop by drop, slowly. When Mike at last swallowed, the kiss grew in heat and passion, their movements becoming liquid.

It couldn't be determined if Mike pushed Chase over on the couch or if Chase pulled Mike down on top of him, but at last they found themselves prone on the old leather sofa.

Mike stretched out on top of Chase, his lips and tongue locked in feverish connection. Their bodies meshed everywhere, and the hardness of their arousal was like a hunger as they ground their hips into each other, helpless to fight the waves of passion cascading over each of them. Conscious thought made a quiet, but determined, retreat. Physical need and instinct stepped in to take its place.

Hands touched, probed, stroked. Arms gripped. Chests, stomach, thighs, and crotches nearly fused in a timeless, primal need to become one.

After a while, Mike lifted his head, pulling his mouth away from Chase's reluctantly. He didn't say anything, but there was a question on his face, and Chase nodded.

Swiftly, they got up from the couch, drained their wineglasses, and headed toward Mike's bedroom. Almost as an afterthought, Chase hurried back and grabbed the wine bottle and their glasses. They laughed.

The bedroom was dark and the pair didn't bring any candles. But the room had a big picture window that faced the dark woods. Rain slashed against the glass, making the forest look like something out of an old black-and-white movie when the lightning flashed. There was something almost unreal about the storm and the wind outside, something that intensified the feeling of closeness and heat inside.

Mike threw back the quilt and top sheet. They undressed quickly in the dark, Mike pausing to grope in his bag for condoms and lube. Chase positioned himself on the bed, biting his lower lip, feeling almost queasy with desire. He raised his legs at the knee, watching Mike finish undressing.

Even in the darkness, it was clear the man was a stunning example of virility, his firm muscles covered with a thin coat of black hair. His cock, fully engorged, rose from between his thighs. Chase got quickly to his hands and knees and headed for the edge of the bed. Mike, standing, moved into position in front of him, cock level with Chase's face. He greedily and without hesitation took Mike in his mouth and throat with one fluid gulp, his lust removing any obstacles. Mike sucked in a breath. Chase began moving his head up and down on Mike's cock, swirling his tongue around the shaft, darting it into Mike's piss slit to taste the precome building up there. He swallowed Mike's cock down so far that it hit the back of his throat and his nose was buried in the coarse curls of Mike's pubic hair. He licked Mike's balls and took them one by one into his mouth, delicately sucking and gently biting at the loose skin. He licked beneath the balls, then reached up and used Mike's hips to turn him around, so that he faced away from Chase.

Chase buried his face in the cleft between Mike's ass cheeks, laving the tight ring of muscle with spit, pushing the tip of his tongue into Mike's hole. Mike quivered and Chase could tell he was getting weak in the knees. He tongue fucked his hole until Mike was panting, groaning, until he was beyond words.

Then Mike turned around, grabbed Chase's head in both of his hands, and slid his cock deep into his throat. He fucked Chase's face almost ruthlessly, but there was no sign from Chase that Mike needed to take heed. In fact, he met Mike's thrusts with a hungry intensity, pumping his own cock almost savagely as he worked.

Chase could feel Mike's balls tightening, his breath quickening, and Chase pulled his head away. A flash of lightning illuminated the beautiful view of Mike's cock, thick, veined and slick with sweat and precome.

"Not so fast," Chase whispered. He scooted back on the bed, pulling a pillow under his head, and placing another under his ass. He raised his legs in the air and looked at his old friend with plaintive eyes.

Mike knelt on the bed and started to lower his face down to Chase's ass, but Chase pulled him away. "No. Just fuck me."

Quickly, Mike tore open a condom wrapper with his teeth, spitting the foil over the edge of the bed. Chase watched from between his thighs as Mike sheathed his cock in latex, then slicked it with lube.

Mike slid a cool dollop of the stuff between Chase's cheeks, worked it in with one finger and then two, working his fingers deeper inside, thrusting faster and faster, until finally four fingers were buried in Chase's chute. "Damn it, Mike. I want your dick!" Chase pulled Mike's hand away from his ass and whimpered, "Please."

Mike positioned himself between Chase's thighs, his cock pressed against his crack, tenderly placing Chase's legs on his strong shoulders. He leaned in, kissing Chase deeply and grabbing his wrists to hold both of his arms behind his head. Mike used his hips to guide himself in, and Chase met him, in a slow, electric connection. Inch by inch, Mike buried himself inside Chase, both men sucking in air until Mike's cock was totally buried.

Their eyes met at that moment and both sighed. "Oh my fuckin' God," Mike whimpered. "I had no idea." He began to thrust, slowly at first, making sure Chase always wanted more, more.

And Chase did. His hips rose to meet Mike's thrusts, his ass clenched down on the thick cock, milking it and making Mike groan with pleasure. They went on for a long time, panting, crying out into the darkness, fucking harder and harder, the intensity and sweat building. Mike pulled out, rolled Chase over on his side and engulfed him in his arms, spoon fashion, then slid back in, bucking against Chase's back as his murmurs and cries of pleasure urged him on, one hand tweaking Chase's nipples while the other stroked his cock. Mike bit down hard on the nape of Chase's neck, twisting his nipple, and felt his hand covered with a flood of hot come just before his own cock erupted deep inside Chase.

They lay like that for a long time, breathing hard, until the storm slowed to a gentle pattering on the windows, until the sweat on their bodies, still pressed together, dried.

Neither said anything. After a while, Chase could tell from the quality of Mike's breathing that he had fallen asleep.

Gently, Chase disengaged and rolled from the bed. He tiptoed from the room and went to his own room down the hall.

He sat naked on the edge of the bed, shivering, and felt like he had just betrayed the only man he had ever loved. He ducked into the adjoining bathroom and took a long shower, letting the water, almost too hot, sluice over him.

Back in the bedroom, he slid under the covers, sure he'd spend the night tossing and turning, enmeshed in guilt.

Instead, within just a very few minutes, his eyelids fluttered and he drifted off, enveloped in a warm cocoon that was like a cloud.


*They're in a church. Probably a Catholic one, because there's the scent of incense in the air, statues of Mary, her hands beckoning, and Christ on the cross.*

*Chase sits across from Toby in a pew. He doesn't dare look at him, certain he's seen what he and Mike did earlier.*

*He starts to speak, to console, to apologize, to explain.*

*But Toby just shoots a quick glance at him. He raises his forefinger to his lips to silence Chase.*

*The words die on Chase's lips.*

*He watches as Toby rises. He doesn't genuflect when he leaves the pew, doesn't bow to the altar. He simply turns and walks back to where Chase assumes the exit is.*

*In the vestibule, Toby's lost in the shadows, swallowed up by the darkness.*

*There's the sound of the door creaking open, a soft thud as it closes.*

*And, all at once, Chase is lying next to Mike, in his bed, as the rain pours down outside.*

*Mike hugs him. "You're a blessing," he whispers. "This is all a blessing."*

*Chase sits up, the sheets slithering from his torso. He turns and looks toward the window.*

*Toby watches from outside.*

*His face is serene.*

Chase woke with a feeling of calmness blanketing him just as much as the quilt covering him.

He could almost feel Toby's presence in bed with him. There was no shame, no guilt. The notion of betrayal was fake.

It was okay.

# Chapter Fourteen

Chase believed he would never fall back to sleep that night. He wanted to hang on to the feeling of Toby beside him and, just as much, wanted to get up and pad to the bedroom next door and climb back into bed with Mike, so they could spoon until dawn's wan light crept into the room.

Remorse? It was gone, despite his sore ass. Questions about loyalty and appropriateness no longer tormented him. For the longest time, he simply lay in bed, staring up at the ceiling. This was something new, something he hadn't experienced since Toby's tragic and final birthday.

And yet...and yet, he had to wonder if he might not be better off simply convincing Mike to drive him back to the city in the morning, so he could return to his original plan of getting an early flight home to Seattle. Yes, their passion and being together had been wonderful and *not* wrong, but there remained so much to think about.

*Am I ready for this? Am I ready for Mike?*

Chase wondered if he should listen to his head—or his heart.

He could tell Mike in the morning he wanted to head back to Seattle. Mike would be disappointed, Chase was certain, but he would understand. And what happened with them tonight? Although Chase couldn't deny the sex had meant a lot to him on an emotional as well as a physical level, he assumed the same might not be true for

Mike. Mike, as Chase had learned time and time again through the years, was an insatiable horn dog, and an evening like tonight, ripe with sexual possibilities, was most likely too alluring for Mike to resist.

Chase could have been anyone...anyone with a penis.

He shook his head. And the shame that rose up had nothing to do with Toby this time or guilt about betraying their love. It had to do with thinking less of the man who was here now, alive, and who obviously cared a great deal about Chase.

*Is that really all you think of Mike?* The question popped into his head from out of nowhere, almost as if his own mind hadn't formed it. Chase turned on his side, staring out at the night, the pale blue-gray clouds that promised the next day would be a rainy one.

Finally, the wine, fatigue from the day, and the sex got to him once again and led him into a fitful sleep.

And then another dream came on the heels of the first. The weird thing about this one was that Chase felt aware of his dreaming, as though he was more observer than participant.

First there was silence, then the ticking of a clock. He was at Toby's fortieth birthday party, and a weird conscious part of him understood he was still in blissful ignorance, that his partner's fateful phone call had yet to come, that Toby's final words, so innocent, were yet to come to him.

"Where can he be?" Chase wondered to Mike. "That man would be late to his own funeral."

The two men laughed, and again Chase's conscious mind intruded to ask if he had really said that bit about Toby's funeral. Too prescient to be credible?

The party continued, and Chase watched a couple guys swaying to Patti LaBelle singing "Lady Marmalade." Toby's sister softly sang along.

Chase's cell phone rang. He froze. Someone shut off the music and, indeed, all sound at the party ceased.

And the device, an iPhone, grew larger so that it was the size of a shoebox. With difficulty, Chase lifted it, the only sound in the room now his thudding heart.

The phone morphed back to its normal size. A horrible sense of dread arose, like something black and monstrous lurking in the shadows but climbing out. He hit Accept and waited. At first, there was only the sound of the wind, and then of traffic.

Time shifted back to clear memory.

Toby was telling him he was home and was just getting off his bus. He was explaining once more how grateful he was for Chase not making a big deal out of his milestone birthday. He so looked forward to a quiet evening at home with the man he loved.

Chase wanted to cling to that voice, so alive, so real. Panic hit him as he realized what was about to happen. His dream shifted from reality to an altered state, where Chase really believed he could change what was about to happen. Maybe this dream was his chance? Maybe if he simply believed hard enough he could alter the past?

If only he could run fast enough, get outside and force Toby not to cross the street at that particular moment in time everything would be changed forever.

His legs felt heavy and leaden, as though he couldn't move fast enough. He made his way down the stairs with effort, since it seemed the distance from his door to the lobby kept doubling, stretching. Finally, he was in the black-and-white tiled lobby with his hand on the brass doorknob.

He rushed outside into the sound of people talking, traffic, and wind. A can skittered along the sidewalk and someone honked a horn.

Chase closed his eyes, for just a fraction of a second, because he was grateful.

There was his Toby across the street! He appeared worn out from the day, wilted, the phone to his ear. His striped tie was loose around his neck. He wasn't paying attention as he talked with Chase, not realizing Chase stood right there, across from him.

Chase turned to his left and saw the white Escalade, heading down the street much too fast. Toby was laughing, intent on his conversation, stepping into the roadway.

Chase opened his mouth to scream, but no voice would emerge. In fact, all the sounds around him stopped as one. He gripped himself, frustrated, angry.

And then, as though some connection had been remade, his voice erupted, loud and panicked. "Toby! Wait! Look where you're going, sweetheart! It's not too late!"

There was a screeching of brakes and the Escalade swerved dangerously close as Toby jumped back. Chase swore he could feel the breeze from the SUV as it whizzed by. Someone called the driver an asshole.

Chase closed his eyes once more, dreading the moment when he would open them again and reality would intrude. Toby's broken, lifeless body would lie on the asphalt before him just as it had on that fateful day. Only this time, instead of viewing it from the distance of their condo window, he would be seeing things up close—the broken body of his love, the shattering of their dreams and future.

But when he opened his eyes, there was Toby, standing across the road from him.

Alive.

Whole.

Well.

Smiling.

And Toby playfully whacked himself on the side of the head for not being more careful about where he was going.

Toby waited for a break in the traffic. Chase thought: *this isn't a dream. It's real. My Toby is alive!* Toby jogged across the street when the roadway was clear and then stood next to Chase, grinning.

"I could have been roadkill. I am such an idiot. You've told me time and again to pay attention when I'm using my phone outside. Thanks for the warning."

Chase couldn't speak. He simply gathered Toby into his arms, pulling him close in an almost viselike grip, inhaling his essence, feeling Toby's stubble on his neck, the very solidity of his body next to his own.

Joy—there was no other word for it.

Finally, Chase pulled himself away reluctantly. He tugged at Toby's hand to lead him back toward the condo, but his partner didn't move.

"Come on, honey. Everyone's waiting. I know you didn't want it, but I made a surprise party for you. Mike came all the way from Chicago." He was so relieved. He no longer cared about the surprise element of the party.

But Toby stayed put. He pulled his hand out of Chase's grasp. There was something sweet and sad creasing his handsome features.

"What?" Chase asked, although a deeper, more primal part of him sensed he already knew.

Toby licked his lips and said, "Chase, you have to learn. You can't change the past. But you *can* make a future." He touched the tip of Chase's nose.

A bus, different from the typical Seattle city buses, pulled up behind Toby. This one was all white, with no lettering or ads. The windows were fogged with condensation. Toby smiled and turned. The bus's doors hissed open, and he boarded.

Chase watched as Toby's blurred silhouette moved to take a seat at the back.

After sitting, Toby drew a heart in the steam on the window.

The bus roared away.

Chase woke to bright sunlight streaming in through the window. Outside, birds chattered. It would not be a rainy day, after all.

Chase's head lolled on the pillow. Instead of feeling fatigued from his restless night, he was recharged, refreshed. He was hungry. He wanted pancakes.

Toby had visited him in the second dream. It wasn't a product of his subconscious.

There are things we know in our hearts when they're real, and Toby's appearance in Chase's slumber was not a phantom of a tortured imagination or a fervent wish, but a visitation. Chase knew it down to his very core.

Toby had a message for him—treasure the past, the joy of it and the memories, but don't let it stand in the way of the future.

*Life.*

He sat up. The day outside looked newly washed. He got up and opened the window, and the fresh morning scent, clean and unspoiled, wafted in. The rain had made everything sparkle in its lemon-yellow light. The grass and leaves on the trees glowed a more intense green. Birdsong filled the air.

He threw the quilt over his bed, stretched, and went down the hall.

He pushed Mike's door open and paused in the doorway to take in a lovely picture—Mike asleep. He lay on his back with one arm thrown over his forehead. The sheet twisted around his strong, hairy legs, concealing one and exposing the other. The top of his cock peeked out, half erect. Despite the carnal image, his face, in repose, was a study in satisfied innocence.

Chase padded to the bed silently and slid in beside Mike. Mike stirred and the arm across his forehead slid over Chase's chest. He pulled Chase close without ever opening his eyes.

It felt right. Meant to be. Real. Good.

Mike mumbled something unintelligible in Chase's ear, his breath hot. Chase nestled into the crook of Mike's arm and shoulder, laying his head on the furry mat of his chest. And then it came to Chase, the word Mike had mumbled.

*Home.*

# About the Author

**Real Men. True Love.**

Rick R. Reed is an award-winning and bestselling author of more than fifty works of published fiction. He is a Lambda Literary Award finalist. *Entertainment Weekly* has described his work as "heartrending and sensitive." *Lambda Literary* has called him: "A writer that doesn't disappoint..." Find him at www.rickrreedreality.blogspot.com. Rick lives in Palm Springs, CA, with his husband, Bruce, and their fierce Chihuahua/Shiba Inu mix, Kodi.

Email: rickrreedbooks@gmail.com

Facebook: www.facebook.com/rickrreedbooks

Twitter: @rickrreed

## Other NineStar books by this author

*Unraveling*

*Sky Full of Mysteries*

*The Perils of Intimacy*

*IM*

*Chaser*

*Raining Men*

*Blue Umbrella Sky*

Also Available from NineStar Press

Connect with NineStar Press

www.ninestarpress.com

www.facebook.com/ninestarpress

www.facebook.com/groups/NineStarNiche

www.twitter.com/ninestarpress